I0665425

HALF PAST SATAN

RICHARD TORONTO

✳ A FRISCO DETECTIVE MYSTERY ✳

ATOMIC CRIME LIBRARY
— San Francisco —

SETTINGS FOR THE STORY IN

HALF PAST SATAN

Omenon Bunker

Shipwreck Cemetery

Pt. Reyes Lighthouse

Bolinas

Pt. Reyes, California

HALF PAST SATAN

Persons this *Mystery* is about—

ALEXANDER "BUSTER" BLADE,

former Hollywood silent film icon known as the Wonder Boy of the Westerns, starts a detective agency after the War, but his latest client is already dead, and wants to communicate through an Ouija board that brings Blade nothing but trouble.

PALOMA LIU TSONG,

Alex Blade's savvy, curvy, part-time assistant and Chinatown exotic dancer, thinks she knows the ins and outs of Ouija boards, but reconsiders her prowess when she finds out bats come from her talking board séances.

LT. LEROY ST. JAMES,

is the stylish, narcissistic, Beethoven-loving cop who worked with Blade on the SFPD before the War, but now that Blade is a private dick, he won't give him an even break. In this episode, St. James falls for a movie icon.

FRANTICEK DRTIKOL, AKA ANANDA VEDANTA,

was a washed up, seven-foot tall pulp fiction writer until he met a source of cosmic information that transformed him into the guru of a death cult bent on ruling the world.

CHIEF JOSEPH IRON LUNG,

a native shaman hired to exorcise the evil spirit haunting Blade's office ends up working for a mythical creature that rescued his tribe from certain death thousands of years ago.

SUS SISTINNAKO,

the thing that came from outer space and got into hot water by reading too many pulp magazines.

DR. ROSWELL DVORAK,

noted UC Berkeley sociologist died in a tragic auto accident but not before leaving behind a letter demanding his killer be brought to justice.

ISABELLE DVORAK,

the Professor's sexy young daughter can't keep her hands off Blade. That makes it hard for him to concentrate on the case, which has more bodies to worry about than hers.

STAN RAYCRAFT,

investigative reporter at the *San Francisco Call-Bulletin* elbows in on Blade's latest case to become a team player, in between Christmas party punch bowls.

BOOKS BY RICHARD TORONTO

War Over Lemuria (2013)
Shaverology – A Shaver Mystery Home Companion (2013)
Shavertron – The Mimeograph Years (2013)
Shavertron – The MacPlus Years (2014)
Shavertron – The Lettershop Years (2014)
Shavertron – The Mimeograph Years (2014)
Rokfogo – The Mysterious Pre-Deluge Art of
Richard S. Shaver, vols. 1 & 2 (2014)
Hollywood and Vain – A Frisco Detective Mystery (2025)
(published in 2020 as Cold War Hot Lead under pseud-
onym Mace Palmer)
Nudist Camp Confidential (2025)
Doom Town and the Atomic Blonde from Sector 9 (2026)

Copyright @2022 by Richard Toronto
Formerly published as Cold War Hot Lead in 2022 under
pseudonym Mace Palmer

Atomic Crime Library by arrangement with Shavertron Press
San Francisco, California

All rights reserved

No part of this publication may be reproduced, distributed,
or transmitted in any form or by any means, including photo-
copying, recording, or other electronic or mechanical methods,
without the prior written permission of the publisher, except
as permitted by U.S. copyright law. For permission requests,
contact friscodetective@gmail.com.

The story, all names, and incidents portrayed in this production
are fictitious. No identification with actual persons (living or
deceased), should be inferred.

Map art: Musicmaster

Cover and interior illustrations: R. Toronto & Dall-e 3 in Photo-
shop

Design and layout by Lora Santiago

Second edition, 2025

1
Fu Chan

Paloma Liu Tsong turned up the radio to cover the high-pitched whine of the dental drill. It echoed through the fourth-floor of the Mayfair Building like a hungry mosquito. The offending buzz came from the office of Dr. Painless Parker, DDS, as he made dental magic—at bargain basement prices—on a customer's throbbing tooth.

Paloma clapped her hands against her ears to shut out the sound.

"That drill gives me the screaming meemies!" she shivered.

She fiddled with the Zenith's dial and tuned in KLX, where Gene Autry was crooning "Here Comes Santa Claus" from high atop the Oakland Tribune Tower.

Paloma is my office assistant. She's half Chinese and half Spanish and she's as smart as she is a knockout. For the mere price of the cover charge at Andy Wong's Sky Room, you can ogle her ample charms as naked as the day she was born, dancing with two ostrich feather fans or a giant bubble. Even when she pours herself into the Venetian twill business suit she wears around the office, there's no way she can hide those curves.

The problem is the dental drill. It gives her goose bumps on her goose bumps. To make matters worse, Dr. Parker was peddling his annual two-for-one Christmas sale on mercury fillings. This year he purchased a quarter-page ad in the San Francisco Chronicle. The ad, as always, warbled like a canary on nitrous oxide.

"San Francisco! Say Hello to 1950 with a healthy smile and a brand new dental filling! Did you know that 70 million new cavities occur in the teeth of adults in the United States each year? Dr. Painless Parker can help! Buy one filling and the second one is FREE! Dr. Parker dares the competition to beat his prices! Enjoy a cavity free Christmas! Call Garfield 5-9977."

Yes, Christmas. It was spreading throughout the shire like a festive case of whooping cough. I could do without it. This time of year, cash-ridden clients looking for private snoops like me are as scarce as a lump of coal in Bob Cratchit's Christmas stocking.

The citizens of our fair city had other fish to fry, like gift shopping and dental work, which explained why I was on a skip trace job in the Tenderloin, gumshoeing my way to cover this month's payment to Ray Chung's TV Bazaar.

At Paloma's urging—against my better judgement—I had traded in our 1947 Dumont set for a top-of-the-line, 1950 Admiral, the model with the faux wood Bakelite cabinet. The upgrade from the round, 10-inch dinner plate screen to a modern, 12-inch rectangle kept peace around the office, meaning, it kept Paloma happy, and when Paloma's happy, life is a lot easier.

While I was wandering the mean streets of San Francisco, Paloma was in charge of the office. The door still had my name on it: Alexander Blade—Confidential Investigations. I'm the guy who pays the rent. We're discreetly located in the Mayfair Building above the Stockton Street tunnel on Bush, one block from Chinatown.

The Chinese generally don't celebrate Christmas, seeing as how Jesus never rode his mule as far as China. Ergo, one might assume Chinatown would be as dead as a Peking duck at this time of year. Not so.

Chinese shop owners are more than happy to cater to any holiday where Occidentals spend greenbacks like drunken sailors, and that

included Christmas. In fact, Chinatown was buzzing with festive holiday shoppers, scurrying thither and hither in that familiar holiday dash the baby Jesus knew nothing about.

Back at Confidential Investigations, Paloma was still trying to stifle Dr. Parker's mechanical mosquito when a well-dressed Chinese, somewhat middle-aged, stepped into the office. Unless he was looking for dental work, he was a potential customer.

The radio had just swapped one cowboy crooner for another. Frankie Laine was straining his tonsils over his new hit single, "Mule Train," with realistic whip snaps between stanzas.

A mustache adorned the upper lip of the man's pale, yellow face. He wore a neatly pressed, dark gray double-breasted Brooks Brothers suit, a light gray "Nob Hill" hat by Knox, and a silk tie in shades of red. Small-boned, with skin as smooth as marble, he seemed nervous, wary of his surroundings. And when he spoke, the words tumbled out in Chinese.

"Nǐ shì zài zhèlǐ gōngzuò de zhōngguó rén ma?" he asked.

Paloma, being California Chinese, replied in California lingo.

"Yes, I am Liu Tsong," she replied.

The man shifted mental gears and replied in perfect English.

"I wish to speak with you on a matter of great urgency. May I sit down?"

KLX had just swapped one cowboy crooner for another. Frankie Laine was straining his tonsils over his new hit single, "Mule Train," with realistic whip snaps between stanzas.

"How rude of me," Paloma said, as she turned off the radio. "Please do. How may I help you?"

"My name is Fu Chan," the man explained. "My late employer was the honorable Dr. Roswell Dvorak, PhD, a sociology professor at UC Berkeley. He has, posthumously I'm afraid, instructed me to engage the services of a private investigator.

"However, on checking the Chinatown telephone directory, I found no Chinese service of this kind. Then I heard of your agency, and that a Chinese worked here, so I came to find out if it were true. It is! You are Chinese."

"I'm half Chinese, Fu Chan. My mother is of Spanish heritage."

"I see. In that case, I wish to speak with your honorable father's half, please."

Paloma's full, red lips smiled.

"I see. Well, Mr. Blade is our operative, and handles all our cases. But he's not in at the moment. However, I'm in charge while he's away. Tell me what brings you here and I'll be happy to discuss it with him when he returns."

"Very well," Fu Chan agreed. Taking a deep breath, he began to unravel a strange ball of yarn.

"Dr. Dvorak left explicit instructions addressed for me in a letter he kept locked in his desk. I was to open it only if his life came to a violent end, which it has. I opened the letter, and found his final instructions. I am to hire a detective to find his murderer and bring him to justice. He enclosed a signed check for one thousand dollars as a retainer. I am to give it to the person capable of granting this final wish. There was also mention of payment for daily expenses. I am to see to that."

"You mean your boss knew he might get beefed? I mean, murdered?" Paloma gasped.

"Yes. It happened while he was driving the coast highway. His car veered across the road, and went over the cliff at Gray Whale Cove. His car burst into flames on the rocks below. Both he and his car were burned beyond recognition.

"The police interviewed a service station attendant in Half Moon Bay who said he had filled the Professor's car with gas shortly before the crash. After a very short investigation, the authorities concluded it was an accident. They have closed the case."

"Did your employer say anything else in this letter?"

"Yes, and this is most important."

Fu Chan reached beside his chair for his leather Gladstone, which he placed on his lap. He unfastened the clasp and pulled out an Ouija board.

"You must communicate with my late employer through this talking board, as stipulated in his last wishes."

"A weejee board? You mean Dr. Dvorak is going to speak to us through this board?"

Fu Chan nodded solemnly. "That was his intention. I know nothing of such matters, but he designated a code word he will use during each session to verify his true identity. The word is 'Marin.' Are you capable of such other-worldly communications?"

Paloma thought fast. Of course she wanted Fu Chan's fat retainer.

"I'm familiar with metaphysical practices, Fu Chan, mostly those of the Far East. However, Mr. Blade has read all 876 pages of the OAHSPE bible. Beings from another planet dictated it through a medium here on Earth. I'm sure Mr. Blade will know how to handle this case."

"I have not heard of OAHSPE, but 876 pages does sound impressive," admitted Fu Chan. "Then you will accept my late employer's proposition?"

"You bet! I mean, yes, of course, Fu Chan. Let me type up a receipt for your retainer."

Paloma could not believe her good fortune, and she took credit for it, too, since it was her idea to build our office shrine to Money God. It finally paid off, she thought.

Visibly more relaxed now, Fu Chan exhaled.

"It is a great relief knowing that a Chinese will handle the Professor's affairs. You may contact me at China 5-6321. Here is my card. I live in Chinatown, of course. As you well know, we Chinese must all live here in Chinatown."

Fu Chan gave Paloma his card, typeset in tidy Futura Narrow. In return, she gave him a typed receipt. He put the receipt in his Gladstone, but left the Ouija board on her desk. As he reached the office door, he turned back.

"Xièxiè nín de bāngzhù, liú cōng. " he said.

"You are most welcome, Fu Chan," Paloma replied.

2
Naughty Nylons

The California Street cable car crawled up the hill like a stuffed holiday turkey filled with young suburban housewives. Like swallows that return to Capistrano each spring, these birds flock to the City at Christmastime to shop at the big department stores. Macy's, Gump's, The White House, City of Paris; these were their preferred nesting sites.

I stood on the lower step of the uphill end of the car and steadied myself, holding on to a brass pole. That gave me a bird's eye view of female shoppers with snug jersey dresses, shapely gams, and stacks of gift boxes on their laps. They were dames with restless offspring, and from the looks of them, the offspring arrived soon after the war, when returning GIs settled their new brides in the California suburbs.

A boy in a cowboy hat, Hopalong Cassidy sweater, and Roy Rogers boots fired his nickel-plated cap guns at pedestrians trudging up the hill. A little girl began to cry when her dolly fell off her lap and into the street. Her mother, wearing a black pillbox hat with a thin veil covering her face, scolded the girl for being so careless. When the car paused at Stockton Street, I stepped off the car and thanked my lucky stars I was single.

I got an early Christmas present when I entered the lobby of the Mayfair Building. Someone had fixed the elevator, and, wonder of wonders, Johnson J. Johnson, Jr., our sometime elevator operator, was on duty. This meant I could haul my barking dogs to the office without taking the stairs.

Sad to say, the lift was no escape from the holiday hysteria outside. Johnson had strung red crepe paper Christmas bells across the ceiling, and taped a hand drawn snowman to the wall. From a portable radio perched on a three-legged stool on the floor, der Bingle whistled "White Christmas." The bells on the ceiling hit me in the face as I got in. Undeterred, I announced:

"Home, Johnson, and Merry Christmas to you, the Missus, and all the little Johnsons."

Johnson mumbled a few words, crossed himself, and pulled a lever on the control panel. The doors closed with an acrid smell of ozone. We lurched upward, ascending to the fourth floor on the wings of angels. I felt as though I'd entered Valhalla when the doors opened with a grinding, metallic squeal.

Confidential Investigations was still there, but I knew something was up as soon as I stepped through the office door. Paloma was waving her gums at me like she'd found a sale on stiletto heels at Macy's.

The shoulder pads on her tailored suit jacket were wide enough to block traffic on Market Street. She'd updated her hair to the shorter, post-war look, but kept the bangs. She was fanning the air with something that looked like a check.

"You'll never guess what just happened," she gushed with a grin as wide as the MacArthur Tunnel.

"Slow down, Angel, let me guess. Somebody mailed a check to the dentist's office and we got it instead?""

"Damn near, Philo!" she chirped. "This check is from our new client, a deceased Berkeley professor named Roswell Dvorak. Did I mention the check is made out to 'cash' for one thousand box tops?"

"No, you did not. But now that you have, add the good doctor to our Christmas card list for deceased clients. Is it safe to assume that being deceased is the reason he's not here at the moment? In which case, how did his check arrive? Wait! He mailed it by Bony Express."

"Gawd, Alex! You are too corny for words! No, he did not. His manservant Fu Chan brought it."

I was annoying her, but she kept going in spite of me.

"There's more to this check than meets the eye, Alex. You'd better sit down."

My dogs were barking anyway, so I sat. Paloma prattled on about a letter and what was in the letter, and a fiery car crash, and why she had an Ouija board on her desk.

"The Professor gave us a code word so we'd know he's the right spook calling us from the spirit world," she gasped, stopping to take a breath.

I said: "Let's recap this Christmas miracle, Moon Cakes. We've got this new client who died under sketchy circumstances. Now, being dead appears to be an important part of this story. In spite of his existential status, he's going to tell us how to nail his killer using a weejee board connected to his happy hunting ground, or wherever eggheads go when they die. Does that about sum it up?"

"That's it in a nutshell, Sherlock."

"Get that check to the bank ASAP, Angel, before the Professor changes his mind. The problem is, I haven't used a weejee board since I was a tyke."

"It's like riding a bike, Alex. You never forget how."

"That may be," I said, "but after you deposit the check, swing by Berkeley Livingstone's bookshop and pick up a weejee board operator's manual. Take a few bucks out of petty cash."

"You wiped out petty cash when you bought that bottle of Vat 69 last week. But as soon as I deposit Fu Chan's check, we'll be sitting pretty. It'll take a few days to clear, but now that your good pal Berkeley owns The Metaphysical Bookstore, I bet he'd be happy to float credit to his favorite Hollywood kid actor, huh?"

"I refuse to rest on the laurels of my former movie career," I snarled. "If I'd stayed in Hollywood like my pal 'Kookie' McKay, the House on Un-American Activities would have railroaded me like it did him. Those Commie-chasing politicians are a bunch of soulless bastards.

"As you probably do not recall, Kitten, Kookie was a successful screenwriter until some anonymous bozo accused him of being a pinko. That blacklisted him, ruined his career. Kookie's a Good Humor man now, hawking ice cream cones to tourists on Hollywood Boulevard. He's lucky to have a job. I have no regrets about putting Hollywood in the rear-view mirror, kiddo."

"Whatever you say, Alex" Paloma groaned. "Let's see some lettuce."

I dove a mitt into my coat pocket, poking around for some greenery.

"Here's something to cover the book," I said. "If it costs more than this, use your feminine wiles. Meanwhile, I've got a skip trace lead to follow up. We can't let Mr. Chung repo the new TV set, now can we? Just hang the 'Back in Five Minutes' sign on the door. It's Christmas. There's nothing but empty stockings in the waiting room."

"I won't be back in five minutes."

"Nobody knows that but us, Angel. If they're desperate, they'll wait. The lock on the door is still busted. They can let themselves in."

Paloma took the cash and counted it.

"Oh, wow! Two bucks," she sneered, and stuffed the bills into her purse. "Maybe I'll buy a ticket to Acapulco and forget about the book."

"That is not the Christmas spirit, Princess. Don't be so cynical. That's my job. Remember—Santa's making a list."

"Yeah, yeah, and he's checking it twice. I'm outta here, but don't wait up for me."

• • •

Like a slice of overripe baloney, the Metaphysical Bookstore was sandwiched between a Jewish deli on one side and an Italian bakery on the other. The bakery infused a hint of yeastiness to the scent of aged parchment and dry leather that permeated the bookstore. Faced in black tile, the narrow storefront had a tunnel-like entrance, with display windows on either side.

Customers strolling through the glass tunnel could marvel at the latest books on metaphysical conspiracies, written by crackpots with doctorates as phony as the Fiji Mermaid. Some were still trying to unravel Hitler's motive for the war. "The Plan," they called it. One popular theory involved a conspiracy by a group of fallen angels. Every night they beamed God-knows-what into Hitler's ear as he slept, which is crazy because everybody knows Hitler never slept. I don't read this tripe myself. Paloma tells me about it. She falls for it big time.

Berkeley Livingstone was organizing the Manly Palmer Hall section of the Astrology shelf when Paloma waltzed through the front door. Her long skirt had a deep kick pleat that revealed a fetching length of silk stocking. The stockings made a seductive, swishing sound as she came in. Legs like hers were the reason God created silk worms. A black satin ribbon tied under her chin held her dark green Cathay of California cartwheel hat.

The Metaphysical Bookstore was one of Paloma's favorite distractions. Just last week she'd purchased a book about flying saucers by an up-and-coming San Diego medium. During his weekly séances, the medium got updates from a saucer commander who kept a beady eye on planet Earth.

Believe it or not, there are people walking the streets of this very city who claim they've taken a ride in a flying saucer. They've even published books about it. What I'd like to know is, where were these space creatures ten years ago? They're everywhere now. It's Orson Welles' fault. If he hadn't aired that *War of the Worlds* broadcast, there wouldn't be any flying saucers.

"Looking for anything in particular, ma'am?" Berkeley Livingstone warbled from atop his wooden perch. He adjusted his wire frame specs, looked down, and squinted. The svelte figure standing below him slowly came into focus.

"Oh! It's you, Miss Paloma! I didn't recognize you. Welcome back. You look absolutely stunning today, if you don't mind my saying."

"Of course not, Mr. Livingstone. Thank you."

"How's Mr. Buster, our Wonder Boy of the Westerns?" Livingstone prattled. He then began a journey down the well-worn memory hole of his youth. Paloma had heard it all before. "I remember him so vividly from my boyhood days," Livingstone recited. "I would arrive early every Saturday morning at the Rex Theatre—they've renamed it the Roxie now—to get a front row seat for the next chapter of Buster's latest cliff hanger. Ah yes, so many wonderful movies. You're one lucky lady to be working with such a talented fellow."

"You can't imagine how glamorous it is." Paloma's sarcasm sailed unnoticed over Livingstone's balding noodle. "Mr. Livingstone, do you have any books about weejee boards?"

"Is the Pope Catholic? That's a joke. Of course he's Catholic, and yes, I have two shelves of books about talking boards. If you're a beginner, I highly recommend *Ouija Boards for the Millions*, by Aldebaran Von Hoek."

"That sounds too generic," Paloma said. "We've got to communicate with the dead."

"Oh my," the book bender squeaked. "That sounds serious."

With the tip of a red fingernail, Paloma pulled a thin volume from the shelf.

"How about this one?" she trilled. "*Secrets of the Successful Use of the Ouija Board.* That sounds more specific, don't you think?"

Livingstone frowned. "That book was published in 1919. It might be a bit dated for modern tastes."

"Come now, Mr. Livingstone! How much have weejee boards changed in 30 years?"

"You've got me there," Livingstone guffawed. "It's a used copy, too. You can have it for ten cents."

"Sold! And with the dollar and ninety cents I have left I'll take this book about the Lemurians living inside Mt. Shasta. Alex will never know."

She handed the books to Livingstone, who took them behind his oak counter. He began wrapping them in brown butcher paper, tying the package with string unreeled from a cone behind the counter. He talked as he tied.

"By the way, Miss Paloma, I have to congratulate you on your photo spread in the November issue of *Naughty Nylons* magazine. It was stunning, absolutely stunning!"

"Why, Mr. Livingstone! I didn't know you were a *Naughty Nylons* fan."

"Oh yes, I keep copies under the counter for our special clients, and I don't mind telling you, Miss Paloma, your feature was tip top."

"What did you think of the title?"

"Let's see, oh, you mean, 'Private Eyeful?' It was brilliant, absolutely perfect."

"That was my idea," Paloma smiled.

"Really? You always were the creative one. I especially liked the shot of you in the deerstalker hat."

"I wanted it to tie in with my future career as a private investigator. I'm studying for the license exam."

"I'm sure you'll pass with flying colors, Miss Paloma! I'll bet Mr. Blade was pleased as punch when you were crowned Miss Naughty Nylons of 1949," Livingstone beamed.

"Not exactly. Sometimes Alex can be a real prude when he puts his mind to it. It's kinda cute, though. I can make him blush at the drop of a hat. He's just a marshmallow with muscles."

Livingstone finished the package and laid it on the countertop. Gingerly, he slipped a mimeographed sheet of paper under the string.

"About this flyer," he explained, smiling through tea-stained teeth. "It's a calendar of our coming events. Maybe you noticed the stage at the far end of the shop?"

Livingstone pointed to a tiny wooden platform big enough to hold one person and a podium. A row of six folding chairs faced the stage.

"Thursday nights at eight o'clock we have an hour of channeling by Mrs. Aura Raynes. She hosts a question-and-answer session with Ashtar, the Supreme Commander of the Galaxy. Friday is Open Mic Night. You wouldn't believe the speakers we get!"

Paloma replied: "Oh, I think I can. It sounds exciting, Mr. Livingstone, but ..."

Livingstone hadn't finished.

"Then there's Sunday! Sunday is our most exciting program yet. We call it, Séance Sundays with The Chief. That's Chief Joseph Iron Lung, shaman extraordinaire. You and Buster should come."

"Wow, a real shaman, huh?" Paloma gaped. "Why haven't I heard about the Chief before?"

"If you're from San Francisco, you probably haven't. He's new in town," Livingstone explained. "He came to the shop a few weeks ago. Hails from up north. Humboldt County. You know, behind the Redwood Curtain?"

A frown darkened Paloma's pretty pan, like a cloud flitting across the sun.

"I'm afraid Alex doesn't go in for metaphysics," Paloma said. "On the other hand, he has to bone up on weejee boards for a case we're working, so you never know. I'll get him down here one of these days."

3
Beethoven's Birthday

I was near police headquarters when I wrapped up my skip trace job, so I thought I'd pay a visit to Lt. Leroy St. James of the Homicide Squad. The official version of Dvorak's death said it was accidental, but St. James might know something the cops didn't release to the press. St. James and I often worked together when I was a SFPD detective before the war. Maybe he'd give me a break. Then again, he can be a moody bastard. You never knew what to expect from that guy.

I out maneuvered the drunk and disorderly crowd at the front desk to reach the pale green corridor that leads to St. James's office. As I poised my knuckles to rap on his portal, the first few notes of Beethoven's Moonlight Sonata caressed my weary ears. The music came from St. James's portable phonograph, which he kept handy to soothe his foul moods. He had those in spades.

I knocked. No answer. I rapped again, harder this time.

"Begone!" a voice scorched from behind the door. I entered.

"Hi, Lieutenant. Happy Holidays. What's up?"

St. James's mug was as doleful as a potted palm in a flop house. Sweat speckled his bald head, making it glow like a big, bare light bulb. His signature bow tie was crooked, and his starched shirt rumpled. His hefty 250 pounds slumped in his swivel chair like a bag of dirty laundry. This was not the self-assured, well-manicured Leroy St. James I used to know. His blood shot eyes took awhile to focus on me, but when they did, a snarl etched his kisser.

"Well, well. Buster Blade," he grouched. "What a surprise. You're like the Christmas present that goes tick tock under the tree. What's up, you ask? What does it look like, Sherlock?"

"Sounds like the Beethoven therapy hour."

"Your powers of observation amaze me, Hawkshaw. But here's the thing. I'm BUSY, so go away!"

The snarky homicide honcho picked up a stack of record albums from his desk and put them back in alphabetical order on a shelf next to a photogravure of Beethoven tacked to the wall. He returned to his chair and hung the copper's beady eye on me.

"Let me ask you a question, Blade. It's a simple question, so no need to write it down. What day is this?"

I replied: "It's December 16, only eight shopping days until Christmas."

"Yeees, aaand...?"

"And the day after Christmas we return the presents for a refund."

At that, St. James catapulted up, slamming his palms on his coffee-stained desk blotter.

"For Pete's sake, Blade! It's Beethoven's birthday! And, as I'm sure you're aware, it's been a longstanding tradition of mine to take the day off, considering it should be a national holiday. I've written letters to president Truman to that effect. He seems to think that's Germany's decision, the dope.

"But when I got up today I said to myself, 'It's Beethoven's birthday, Leroy. You'd better run down to the office. Buster Blade might drop by to ask me what's up? So, here I am. What's the beef now, Blade? You have a parking ticket you want fixed?"

"Not really. I was in the neighborhood on business, so thought I'd stop by to see how you're getting along, that's all."

St. James sat down, parked his elbows on the desk, resting his chin on his hands. After a moment of silence, his demeanor changed. The boiled pudding that made up his pasty mug settled down. He leaned back in his chair and clasped his hands behind his polished dome.

"This sudden interest in my wellbeing gives me pause," he mused. "It's so, how shall I put it, out of character; and yet, so timely. You want to know how I'm getting along, eh? Okay, I'll tell you. Ludwig and I are brooding, brooding over another dame who done us wrong. Does that surprise you, Sherlock?"

It did. St. James was a confirmed bachelor by all outward appearances. He never discussed his peccadilloes, if there were any, and I'd never seen him on a date. That's when I noticed the photo of Gene Tierney on his desk, a black and white headshot, the kind Hollywood stars send to fans. Someone had torn it into four pieces and then pieced it back together with cellophane tape.

I quipped: "Don't tell me you've fallen for one of the fair sex? I don't believe it."

"Yeah? Well, there's a lot you don't know about me, Blade. It's no secret that I'm a genius in the world of crime fighting. But does that impress the dames? Hardly. All I got from Miss Tierney was a cease and desist letter from her attorney. No matter. It always ends this way, with me howling at the moon over a One-eyed Eskimo frozen dinner."

I couldn't hide my surprise, or my lack of interest in this Gene Tierney delusion.

"Well, I'll be! Another fan of the frozen dinner craze?" I japed. "It's becoming an epidemic. Paloma thinks these new frozen dinners are God's gift to the human race, next to television."

In an instant, St. James' expression pulled a one-eighty. His eyelids fluttered like he'd just snapped out of a trance. He stood up, went to the phonograph, turned off his Beethoven platter, and grabbed his overcoat and derby hat from the wooden stand.

"Okay, Blade, let's have it," he grimaced. "You didn't drop by to write my life story. What do you want? And make it snappy. There's a stiff waiting for me in Dogpatch and my driver gets real edgy when we run late."

"Now that you mention it, there is something that's been bothering me," I said. St. James was already sprinting out the office door, so I paced him and kept yakking.

"What's the scuttlebutt on a Dr. Roswell Dvorak, you know, the guy who drove his car over a cliff at Gray Whale Cove? I mean, aside from, it was an accident?"

"First of all, why would an auto accident interest a private dick? There's no there, *there*, Buster. As far as the San Mateo Sheriff's office is concerned, it was just another tragedy on the Pacific Coast Highway. The driver happened to be a well-known Berkeley professor this time. These things occur every year like clockwork, from Monterey to Bodega Bay."

"I know what the press said," I countered, "but what I need is off-the-record chatter, the kind that would interest a discerning sleuth such as yourself. Some unusual tidbit of information."

"You mean like how the egghead was a member of a goofball cult called Omenon? Is that the tidbit you're after? Forget it! The sheriff checked that angle and found no connection between the cult and Dvorak's death. I'll admit that it was impossible to pull out any serious forensics from the scene. The body was a fried oyster."

"I take it this Omenon cult was already on law enforcement's radar?"

"No shit, Sherlock!" St. James paused at the water cooler, yanked a Dixie cup from the dispenser, and filled it as we watched bubbles gurgle to the top of the glass jug.

"Omenon's founder is a seven foot tall has-been pulp hack named Ananda Vedanta," St. James continued. "He made Marin County his headquarters after moving there from Twenty-nine Palms. He's got a compound near Inverness that's straight out of a Buck Rogers comic strip.

"Omenon filed for church status with the state of California and got it last year. If you ask me, the guy's a grifter, and landed with both feet on a sweet scam. His message is a combination of meditation, Crowleyan magic, and Blavatsky Theosophy. He's schmoozed the local politicians, too. They respect him for taking hopheads off the streets, drying them out, and turning them into tax-paying Omenon citizens. All I can say is there's a sucker born every minute."

"Which makes me wonder," I said, "why would a Berkeley professor join a cult like that?"

"The world is a strange place, Sherlock."

We had reached the curb where a black Ford V-8 sedan with SFPD markings rumbled impatiently.

"Now, go peddle your papers, Philo. I've got real detective work to do, not skip trace jobs like snoops resort to when they run out of frozen dinners."

St. James' sense of humor was about as stale as last year's Christmas candy.

"So, you know about the skip trace job, huh?"

"I'm the world's greatest detective. Jeez, Blade, you should know that by now."

A plainclothes gorilla with mitts as big as wrecking balls opened the rear door of his cruiser. A second primate, with muscles on top of muscles, gripped the steering wheel, staring mindlessly through the windshield. St. James slid into the back seat, and with a roar of its flathead V-8, the cruiser sped off in a cloud of gutter butts and burned rubber. I flicked my butt into the gutter with a hundred others just like it.

4

Talking Boards and Hell Money

Paloma finished the final chapter of her Ouija board book and was jotting down notes when I breached the office door. I closed it quietly behind me.

"Oh, Lotus Flower," I cooed, "if you keep expanding your mind like this, some day it will occur to you there's more to life than fan dancing and sharing office space with a licensed skulk like me."

"Don't be so downbeat," Paloma replied. "You're still my favorite private dick. Besides, sleuthing is my new career. Every girl needs a career, and before you know it, I'll have my PI license. Then we'll be full-fledged partners and I can ditch the naked dancing gig."

"What? No more naked dancing?" I squawked. "You have natural talent for it, in all the right places, too. Since when did this den of debt become your career goal?"

"Since reading Mickey Spillane's *I, the Jury*," she gushed. "Oh, boy, that Mike Hammer! What a hunk!"

"Mike Hammer?" I growled. "He's a joke! How can you take a guy with a name like Mike Hammer seriously?"

"It's a play on words," Paloma explained. "Don't you get it? He hammers women's hormones. Just look at Velda, his secretary. She drools every time he walks in the room. She can't help herself; it's her hammered hormones. Or rather, Mike Hammered hormones."

"So this is how you study for your PI license? Reading Hammer novels?"

"Never you mind how I study," Paloma replied. "It's time to earn Fu Chan's fat retainer. Let's take this weejee board for a spin. You get to ride shotgun. This'll be a piece of cake, and it's bringing in a cool grand."

"Okay, Kitten, you're the expert. Wait. Let me rephrase that. You read the book; we'll see if you pass the test."

"Stop yakking and bring two chairs over here, facing each other."

"Your wish is my command, Princess."

I ankled into the waiting room, picked up a captain's chair with each arm, and arranged them in front of Paloma's desk.

"Now, sit facing me. Scoot up close. C'mon, closer! Our knees have to touch to complete the psychic circuit."

"That's not the only circuit it'll complete," I said. "No wonder these things are so popular."

"Try to relax, Alex. Place the tips of your fingers gently on top of this."

She laid a flat, heart-shaped object made of Bird's-eye maple in the center of the board. It had three tiny footpads, and a circle cut out of the middle.

"This is called a planchette," Paloma explained, as if I wouldn't know, which I didn't. She picked up her book and began reading.

"*One must be possessed of a calm, fair-dealing nature, without violent prejudices, malice or small meanness. The spirit world shuns people with these characteristics*".

"Check," I said. "No small meanness here."

With our fingertips touching the planchette, Paloma began breathing deeply and rhythmically. Her impressive breastworks expanded her form-fitting sweater with every breath, much to my distraction. After a few minutes of this heavy breathing jazz, she spoke. Not to me, to the board.

"Spirit within the board. Can you hear me?"

I felt a gentle tug under my fingers. The planchette edged its way to the word YES on the board.

"Well, I'll be dipped," I croaked. "Did you see that?"

Paloma shushed me. "Quiet! You'll ruin the connection!"

I got light-headed watching Paloma's heavy breathing technique. Then, she dove into the dark waters of the Unknown.

"Are you our spirit contact?"

The planchette ran circles around the board until it stopped at YES.

"Now we're getting somewhere," I whispered. "Tell him we're here to help find out who croaked him. Better yet, ask if he knows who croaked him so we can wrap this up."

"We have to choose words carefully when speaking to the spirit world," Paloma whispered back.

My knees tingled as they warmed on Paloma's showgirl gams. I distracted myself by thinking of Fu Chan's retainer in my bank account. Paloma picked up the conversation with our deceased client.

"Will you let us help you?" she asked.

"YES."

"How can we help you?"

The planchette did a crazy dance across the board, moving from letter to letter. I wrote down each one. "BURN INCENSE," it spelled.

"What in the good sister's classroom is he talking about?" I groused. "What does incense have to do with a murder case?"

Paloma ignored me. She was at one with the board. I guess this is what mediums look like when they encounter citizens from another galaxy.

"Is there anything else you want us to do?" Paloma asked.

The answer to that question took a good five minutes, spelling words letter-by-letter before the planchette finally conked out. The spirit had obviously taken a powder, but not before leaving this message: PAY ONE MILLION HELL MONEY FOR MY RETURN.

Paloma snapped out of her dream state. Eyes wide open now, she beamed: "I told you this would be a cinch."

"That's what bothers me," I frowned. "What's all this malarkey about Hell Money?"

"It's ancient Chinese tradition," Paloma soothed. "Hell Money isn't real money, at least not in this world. You burn it as an offering for a deceased loved one's debts in the afterlife."

"Since when do dead people need cash?"

"Yanlou Wang, Lord of the Earthly Court, judges human souls," Paloma explained. "After his judgment, the deceased person either goes to heaven or is banished to an underworld maze of caverns to atone for his sins. Long story short, spirits need Hell Money to pay their fines in the heavenly court."

"My point is," I grappled, "Roswell Dvorak does not sound like a Chinese name to me. Why does an Occidental need Hell Money?"

"Hard to say, but his manservant, Fu Chan, took care of his daily affairs. Maybe it was Fu Chan's idea."

Before I could protest further, Paloma had me flagging my Florsheims to the nearest Chinese religious supply store for a wad of spirit dough. I didn't have far to flag. There were plenty of shops along Washington Street that sold accessories for the hereafter.

Randomly, I chose Uncle Charlie's Happy-Go-Lucky Gift and Herb Shop. After wading through a dense cloud of incense smoke at the door, I turned out to be the only Occidental bozo in the shop; a solitary sugar cube in a pot of oolong tea. My fellow shoppers hung the sly slant on me whenever they thought I wasn't looking. No doubt they wondered why a cracker was foraging for Chinese Hell Money.

It wasn't long before I found three shelves full of it. The bills featured landscapes, animals, temples, and various Chinese potentates I never heard of. But, in English lettering at the top of each bill was, "Bank of Hell." I grabbed two bundles worth a cool two million Hell bucks. Spirits are a cheap date, I thought, only 20¢ for two million plasters!

5
Not as Easy as it Looks

Someone had hung a Christmas wreath on the office door while I was away. A cluster of silver sleigh bells jingled as I entered. I worked my upper lip into a Scrooge-like sneer.

"Where'd the wreath come from?" I asked.

"Like it?" Paloma chirped.

"About as much as Mother's Day at an orphanage. I assume this Christmas cheer comes from your Latin side. Less than a month ago you had me building a shrine for the lunar New Year. Then it was a shrine for Día de los Muertos."

"That's what's great about us half-breeds," she said. "We get to celebrate twice as many holidays."

"Bah, Humbug!" I snorted, and hobbled into my inner sanctum for a shot of Vat 69.

Paloma yelled after me: "Did you get the Hell Money?"

I drifted back in with a glass in one hand and a bundle of Hell Money in the other. I dropped the Chinese lettuce on her desk and downed my glass of Christmas cheer.

"Okay, Moon Cakes, will that take care of it?"

"That's all we'll need to pay off the Professor's debt to the underworld and then some," she said.

"So, what next? Do we mail it to his post office box in Purgatory?"

"Ha ha, you are so clueless. No, Alex, we burn it on an altar. I'll show you how it's done."

Paloma took the sand-filled incense bowl from Money God's shrine and set it next to an open window. She counted out one million of the bogus bucks, tossed in another $50,000 as a tip for somebody or other, and began folding the bills into orderly shapes. She made a pyre of the folded bills, centering them in the bowl.

She held out her palm. "Got a match, big boy?"

I pulled a matchbox from my coat pocket, took out a stick, and lit it with my thumbnail. She took the match, held it under the pyre, and the folded bills lit up. We stood back and watched a million smackers go up in flames. I wasn't even Chinese, but it still gave me heartburn to watch.

As the last finger of flame died out, we heard what sounded like fluttering above our heads.

"Did you hear that, Alex?" Paloma edged closer, grabbing my arm.

The high-pitched squeal of a bat echoed above our heads. The flying mouse swooped and climbed in figure eights around the room. Paloma reached down and yanked her skirt up and crawled under her desk. This revealed a glorious panorama of creamy thighs, garter belts, and black silk stockings.

"Open a window, shoo it out!" she shrilled.

I launched myself to the storage closet to grab a broom. It took me a good twenty minutes, flailing around the room like a ballerina with a hotfoot, before the winged rodent engaged its radar and sailed through the open window. I slammed the window shut and let out a whistle.

"That was some fun, Legs," I puffed. "Where in blue blazes did that come from?"

I felt my coat pockets, hunting for my pack of Chesterfields. I found it and plugged my kisser with a wheezer.

Exhaling toxic fumes, I asked Paloma, "Am I just imagining it, or was that an odd coincidence? We've never had bats in here, but that one showed up right after you burned that Hell Money. I wonder..."

Paloma hadn't heard a word I'd said. She was too busy reorganizing her feminine underpinnings: adjusting garter belts, pulling down her skirt, closing the curtain on my *Naughty Nylons* cheesecake review.

Calmly, she theorized, "Maybe the bat was part of the process."

"Process? What process?" I yapped. "Maybe we should rethink this talking board business, Legs. Where's that book?"

Paloma pulled it from her desk drawer. I took it, thumbed through the pages. I found what I was looking for on page 32 and began reading.

Another contending force from the great beyond is the unrepentant, evil spirit who is indistinguishable from good spirits only by their terrible faces—faces so evil that at first sight they may be thought of as ogres. These ogres hover about our Earth, coming from the fountainhead of evil, an evil that existed before the construction of our known universe.

I said: "Didn't you tell me the Professor gave us a code word? Where's his letter?"

Paloma hauled her hindquarters to the filing cabinet and pulled the Dvorak file. After a quick scan, she confirmed my suspicion.

"You're right," she said. "The Professor's code word was Marin. There was no mention of Marin during our session. We jumped the gun."

Ah, yes, we jumped the gun. This was shaping up to be a Christmas I wouldn't forget.

"Listen, Legs, get Fu Chan on the blower and set up a conference. I'll put the squeeze on him for more details about this talking board baloney he got us into."

Paloma pulled Fu Chan's business card from the file and dialed his number: China 5-6321. Fu Chan must have picked up because she began talking Chinese lingo lickity split. After a conversation as tough to unravel as my phone cord, she hung up.

"Fu Chan said to meet him at his apartment at two o'clock. He'll wait for you there." Paloma wrote the address on a slip of paper and gave it to me.

"He lives in Spofford Alley," she said. "Thirty-six Spofford Alley, apartment eight."

6
Fu Chan's Unlucky Day

Spofford Alley was like most Chinatown alleys—narrow, dark, and dangerous for private snoops to poke around in. Garments fluttered from clotheslines above the alley like flags for some mysterious Chinese festival.

Number 36 was a narrow storefront painted bright red. The official-looking sign said it was the Ghee Kung Tong Supreme Lodge of Chinese Freemasons of the World. It was a very long sign.

Fu Chan lived in one of the apartments on the second floor above the lodge. I was staring at the red front door, wondering how to get in, when it opened and an ancient Chinaman wearing a black Changshan with gold piping wandered out. I took advantage of his exit. The codger gave me the wary Asiatic stare as I traded places with him. He chose to forget he'd seen me. Minding one's own business was the road to wisdom and long life in Chinatown.

The Ghee Kung Tong apartment building was the kind of place that made me want to run to the firebox if my cigarette ash dropped on the floor. Musty, dead air infused with the scent of steaming bok choy filled my lungs as I began my claustrophobic climb in the dim stairwell.

From behind the door to my right I heard Chinese lingo as hot as a bartender's bunion. The shrillest voice was female. I didn't need to speak Chinese to know she was about to drive home a point with her meat cleaver.

Paloma's note said Fu Chan's apartment was number eight at the end of the hall. I was heading in the right direction.

I knocked at number eight and waited. I knocked again and waited some more. Odd, I thought. Fu Chan said he'd be here. I turned the knob and found the door unlocked. Once inside, I got that prickly feeling on the back of my neck that tells me something's not right. Whenever I entered a cave on Peleliu Island to flush out Jap soldiers during the war I got the same feeling.

"Fu Chan?" I crooned from the entryway. I felt like an extra in an Orson Welles movie. All it needed was Rita Hayworth and her pack of Chinese gangsters to finish the scene.

I pulled my police special from its holster and edged my way into the living room. Like Chinatown, it was a modest room. A rose colored camelback sofa sat against a bay window, with a black lacquered coffee table in front of it. Scenes of Chinese rivers and mountains that were painted on rice paper hung on the walls. A shrine with a laughing Buddha sat in one corner of the room. He was smiling over a bowl of California oranges, neatly stacked into a pyramid.

Fu Chan was here, all right, lying on the floor as dead as my movie career. One mean gorilla had worked him over with the proverbial blunt instrument. Bits of spongy, gray blobs littered the carpet like a stack of Chinese lottery tickets in a tornado.

The tornado also broke a Chinese vase on an end table next to the sofa, smashed a slag glass lamp, and rifled through a China cabinet full of Jingdezhen blue and white rice grain dishes; bowls, plates, tea cups, that sort of thing. It didn't look valuable to me. Something seemed phony about it.

I grabbed the candlestick telephone in a nearby wall niche and hailed the Chinese switchboard. The girl patched me through to Leroy St. James in homicide.

"Lieutenant? Alexander Blade talking. I'm at 36 Spofford Alley, apartment eight. You've got a customer here who's gone to meet his ancestors the hard way. Bring the meat wagon."

St. James gave me his boilerplate warning: "Don't touch anything, and stay put, shamus!"

I disobeyed the first order and checked Fu Chan's coat pockets. No wallet. Then I checked his trouser pockets. I found some change, keys, and still no wallet.

Twenty minutes later, St. James, his two bodyguards, and five harness bulls cordoned off the alley. That put the fear of the heathen gods into every Chinese within a two-block radius. The voices I'd heard on entering the building went as silent as the snow on Mt. Everest. Chinatown has a sixth sense when it comes to coppers. Everyone knows when to disappear.

St. James stood out like a sore thumb in his derby hat, red bow tie, tweed overcoat, and custom made Italian shoes. He'd had his badge fashioned into a belt buckle. Not regulation, but he didn't care.

He walked up to me without salutations and shouted: "Okay, Blade, what now?"

"The victim is Fu Chan, Lieutenant," I quacked. "He worked for the late Dr. Roswell Dvorak. Remember? The guy I was asking you about?"

"Tell me something I don't know, Blade," St. James griped. "Fu Chan attended Dvorak's inquest. What I want to know is, what are *you* doing here?"

"Fu Chan was my client. I see no reason to withhold his name, now that he's dead. Fu Chan was working at the behest of his deceased employer when he hired me."

St. James gave me the hard copper stare.

"Run that by me again, Buster! When exactly did Fu Chan hire you?"

"Three days ago. Beethoven's birthday, when I stopped in to see you."

"You're telling me Dvorak told Fu Chan to hire you after he'd already been dead?"

"It's complicated," I said, torching a Chesterfield. "Dvorak knew there was a pretty good chance he'd be murdered." I exhaled smoke through my nose, staring at my shoes thoughtfully.

"Listen, Philo, this isn't an audition for *Little Women*! Spill your guts, and make it snappy!"

"Okay, okay! When Dvorak was still among the living," I continued, "he left written instructions to hire a private investigator in the event he should die under mysterious circumstances. Fu Chan put me on the job after Dvorak met his maker, see? I was to meet Fu Chan here at two o'clock, to get more details about the case. Someone didn't want him to keep his appointment. That's when I called you."

A frown buckled his otherwise placid, light bulb dome.

"Of course. Next question," St. James droned. "Who beefed Fu Chan?"

"That's easy. It had to be the same perp that killed the Professor. I know, I know! It was an accident, but I'm not as sure of that as you are. It's all coming up murder in my book, at least that's how I'll put it in my diary tonight."

St. James ordered one of his minions to rifle through Fu Chan's pockets. No wallet, no ID. The apartment looked ransacked, in a staged sort of way. St. James turned to face me.

"You don't need a fortune teller to figure out what happened here," he gloated. "Looks like a bungled burglary. They broke in, Fu Chan surprised them, and they clobbered him. His wallet is missing and his apartment's been searched for valuables. There's your motive."

An ambulance shrieked to a stop in front of the Ghee Kung Tong Lodge. I had nothing more to offer; at least, nothing St. James wanted to hear. Far be it from me to argue with the world's greatest living detective.

"Now that you've wrapped up the case," I crooned, edging toward the front door, "feel free to call if I can be of any more help. I'm in the Yellow Pages."

"Your kind of help I don't need," he sniped. "On second thought, do me a favor, Blade."

"What's that?"

"Become a florist, do something useful," he advised. Pointing his chewed stogie at Fu Chan's crumpled remains, he groused: "My calendar only has 365 days, and if I'm a very good boy, some of those are supposed to be days off. I've already missed Beethoven's birthday, fer Christ's sake. Don't keep adding to my workload."

7
Little Pete

It was pretty clear to me we were off to a shaky start. Not only did we not find the egghead in Fu Chan's spook board, we found out another tenant had checked into it. Likely as not, the late Fu Chan was looking for his own a stash of Hell Money by now. I wasn't sure who we were working for, with two clients already dead. To straighten things out, I turned to my talking board expert.

"Okay, Angel," I croaked, "who'd we cremate those million Hell clams to if it wasn't the Professor?"

Paloma had clearly put dark thoughts like that out of her pretty head. She painted a much rosier picture for me.

"I can't be sure who it was, Alex, but *Feng Shui* teaches that finding a bat in the house means there's good *chi*," she smiled. "For us Chinese, that means good fortune. Too bad my European side gets creeped out by bats. To be honest, I don't know what to think."

A heavy thud in my inner sanctum ended our conversation. Peering through the connecting door to the other room, we saw what had made the sound. A hatchet had somehow buried itself in my desk, which was quite a feat, seeing as how it was a Navy surplus desk built to withstand atomic attack. Fu Chan's talking board was vibrating maniacally next to the hatchet.

"Someone wants to speak with us," Paloma said. "We'd better try another session."

"Now, now, Princess! We're pushing our luck. On the other hand, if there's a chance the Professor's on the other end of the wire, we'd better find out."

And so, Paloma began prepping for another round of heavy breathing.

"We have to find out who threw that hatchet," she panted. "Obviously, it's an ethereal object that's transported itself to the physical plane. There's no other explanation."

"Yeah, none. It looks real enough to me."

"That's because it is real, Alex," she replied, trying to maintain composure.

We positioned ourselves in the chairs for another session with Fu Chan's board. Knees in place, fingers on the thingamabob, Paloma began drifting into her trancelike state while I completed the circuit. After more deep breathing, Paloma got to the point.

"To whom am I speaking?" she quavered to the board's homicidal tenant.

The planchette took off in a flash. After a crazy trip around the board, it spelled out a name: "FUNG JING TOY."

My knees felt like they'd turned to rubber.

"That's it, game over," I croaked. "I know that name! Remember I told you my Uncle Jesse ran the Chinatown Squad back in the day? When I was a kid, he used to tell me horror stories about this Fung Jing Toy. Chinatown called him Little Pete. He was so bad, people ran to the other side of the street when they saw him coming.

"During the Tong War days, he was grand poobah of the Som Yop Tong. He finally got his comeuppance when a couple of boo how doy assassins bumped him off while he was getting a shave at a Chinatown barbershop. But that was over 50 years ago. What I want to know is, what's he doing here?"

"I'm afraid we brought him," Paloma sighed. "The Hell Money we burned was his Get Out of Jail Free card. He's returned to his old turf. I suspect that's where the bat came from; Fung Jing Toy's netherworld."

"Remind me to write a letter to Dick Tracy about this." I sneered, "And here I'm the guy who bought the Hell Money to break him out."

As Paloma calculated our negative karma for reviving a deceased highbinder, the television flickered on. We were nowhere near it, but it turned itself on all by it's lonesome. The high-pitched wail of a Chinese opera blared from the speaker, accompanied by screeching violins and crashing cymbals. The picture tube glowed blood red. Seasick green horizontal bars fluttered up and down.

"I hope this thing is still on warranty," I said. "Where's the number for Chung's TV Bazaar? There's something wrong with this television."

The image of an antique Chinaman, clean-shaven, complete with Manchu pigtail and skull cap, materialized on the cathode ray tube. The figure's black, loose-fitting clothing had been the style during Chinatown's Victorian era. He sat, emperor-like, in a barber's chair.

"What the—that's *him*!" I yeeped. "Fung Jing Toy, Little Pete—the terror of the tongs—and he's broadcasting live on my TV set! What gives?"

"I am feeling so much better now," the figure said in unearthly, electronic tones. "You shall be rewarded for your loyalty."

We were dumbstruck. Then Paloma got angry.

"This better not cut into Big Time Wrestling tonight," she snapped.

Paloma had reason to get peeved. She had rescheduled her Wednesday night performances at the Sky Room just so she could watch Big Time Wrestling on TV. It was one of her favorite programs.

Speaking to the sinister figure on the picture tube, I said: "No need for return favors, Pete. Uh, how long will you be staying here in Chinatown?"

The set suddenly went black. Little Pete was gone. How he got from the board into the TV was a mystery, but Pete's presence was escalating faster than we were solving the Dvorak case. I turned to Paloma.

"Legs, we need the Professor pronto, before Little Pete makes an encore. I don't want that gangster high jacking my TV while I'm still on the installment plan!"

Again, we sat in our Ouija board chairs, knees connected, fingers braced on the wooden wordsmith. Paloma was taking those deep breaths that filled her pullover sweater in such delightful ways, and I paid close attention. Finally, she was ready to commune with the world of disembodied spirits. This time, she chose her words with caution.

"We wish to contact Dr. Roswell Dvorak," she announced to the board. "If Professor Dvorak can hear me, please speak now."

Under its own power, the planchette took off, stopping at various letters. The words were:

"DVORAK HERE. IGNORE THE OTHER GUY."

It sounded legit, but I was in no mood to get suckered by another spirit. I said to Paloma:

" Prod him, see if you can get the secret word out of him."

"If this really is Professor Dvorak," she said, "what message would you like to give us?"

"SEE MY DAUGHTER IN MARIN COUNTY."

"That's the Professor!" Paloma yelped. "Marin is the secret word! Fu Chan said Dvorak lived in Marin County in a place called Ross. I'll bet that's where we can contact his daughter."

Paloma grabbed the phone and dialed Information. She got Dvorak's number and called. The gist of the conversation with the person on the other end of the line was that I could meet Isabelle Dvorak tomorrow afternoon at her Marin County digs.

8
Isabelle Dvorak

There were five shopping days left before Christmas as I crossed the Golden Gate Bridge into Sausalito. My Hudson Commodore raced up the Waldo Grade like a squirrel up a telephone pole. Nearing the turnoff to San Quentin, I crossed Corte Madera Creek and entered Greenbrae, where I followed Sir Francis Drake Boulevard for several miles until I reached San Anselmo, a bucolic village with a Romanesque castle on a hilltop. The Presbyterians run a seminary for aspiring theologians there.

I took a hard left on Bolinas Avenue, a quiet, tree-lined street that hadn't changed much since the Gay Nineties. Two and three-story Victorians with gingerbread trim and weathervanes on the roof lined the street. Holiday garlands festooned front porch railings. Douglass fir trees with blown glass ornaments sparkled behind parlor windows and white picket fences. The scent of oak, redwood, and bay laurel trees wafted through the Hudson's cowl vent and made me giddy. Frisco, this was not.

Turning onto Greenwood, I drove into the heart of Ross, where society's upper crust cocooned itself behind thick box hedges. This was old money that left San Francisco after the '06 Quake, seeking refuge in the bucolic country. To gain access to one of these hidden estates, you must pass through a locked gate, opened by appointment only.

I found the Professor's stately wigwam and reined in the Hudson. Next to the wrought iron gate, a brick column with a speaker and a big, white button looked like the preferred method of communication. I stretched my arm out the car window and pushed the big, white button.

"Alexander Blade to see Miss Dvorak," I squawked.

I waited in stately silence. Birds chirped and rustled in the hedgerows. It was unnerving. I'd already quaffed half my coffin nail when a voice came through the speaker. A woman with a heavy Chinese accent said:

"You may drive in, Meestah Blade."

The whirring of an electric motor followed, and the gate began a slow swing inward.

I aimed the coupe's hood ornament up the wide brick driveway until a Craftsman mansion in the Julia Morgan style came into view. Maybe it was a Julia Morgan. It had deep, overhanging eaves, walls covered in brown shingles, and an expansive front porch with thick, white columns.

I dropped anchor next to a yellow '48 Packard convertible and crushed my wheezer in the dashboard ashtray. It was so full of butts I could barely squeeze it in. One of these days I'll empty it in front of police headquarters.

At the top of the wide staircase, I came to an equally wide front door painted red. A Chinese maid opened it.

"Alexander Blade to see Miss Dvorak." I was repeating myself, but it was the best I could do.

"Missy expecting you," the maid replied with the same accent I heard over the speaker. "I am Mai Ling. Follow me, please."

We ankled over Persian rugs, past marble statues, and furniture built for people who lived on top of giant beanstalks. She took me to the library, judging from the rows of books that lined the walls.

"Missy will see you shortly, please," Mai Ling said. "Making yourself comfortable, please. Thank you so much." She closed two pocket doors as tall as Paul Bunyon, as she backed ingratiatingly out of the room. I was alone with wall-to-wall books and a collection of framed photos. I went for the photos.

Aside from Ivy League rowing team shots, European vacations, chess matches, and goofy shots of university eggheads, there was a photo that didn't fit. I assumed one of the men in the picture was Professor Dvorak. He stood next to an extremely tall, thin man wearing a rustic robe, long hair, and chin whiskers. The Prof beamed at the camera as he and the scruffy-looking hermit shook hands in front of an enormous portrait of the hermit, large enough to view from the moon. The Bohemian bozo in the robe must be the Ananda Vedanta joker Leroy St. James told me about.

As I studied the photo, a voice like glass wind chimes tinkled behind me: "The one of the naked baby on the bear rug is me."

I turned to look. Leaning against a doorjamb on the other side of the room stood a bundle of femininity hotter than a hockshop handgun. She looked about twenty, but could have been younger. Blonde, blue-eyed, she wore a short-sleeved white sweater that clung to her curves like a barfly to her last drink at closing time. Below her sweater was a tennis skirt so short I didn't need my imagination to see what was under it.

I knew I was staring, but I couldn't help it. My glazed optics caressed her perfect legs all the way down to her white tennis shoes. Sweat glistened on her pale, ivory skin. She was slightly out of breath, and holding a tennis racket. Her limp, bobbed hair hung just below her chin.

I felt all warm and fuzzy inside, like grilled cheese. On her advice, I studied her baby picture.

"You've filled out in all the right places," I quipped.

"I'm Isabelle. Sorry I'm late. I was hitting a few balls out on the court."

I wondered whose balls, but what I said was:

"It was worth the wait. I had time to look at your family's rogue gallery."

"Please, call me Belle," she said. "I don't go in for that 'Miss Dvorak' jazz. Can I tell you a secret?"

"If it includes me."

"You're the first private dick I've ever met. Are they all as well appointed as you?"

"Not usually. I take vitamins."

The one of the naked baby on the bear rug is me.

"A sense of humor. I like that," she smiled down from her cloud. "I understand Fu Chan hired you to look into Father's death. I don't understand it. He died in an auto accident. The case was closed after the inquest."

"My condolences about your father, but Fu Chan believed it wasn't an accident. Oh, About Fu Chan; I'm afraid I have bad news. He died yesterday."

The Dvorak damsel's tennis racket hit the floor. Stunned, she pushed her hair back with both hands in disbelief.

"Fu Chan, dead? He looked perfectly healthy when I saw him last week."

"That was before a blunt instrument wafted him to his ancestors," I replied. "It was murder."

"That's horrible! He and Father were so close. Now they're both gone."

"Did you know about a letter your father addressed to Fu Chan, to be opened in the event of his death?"

"Yes, yes, I knew all about that. Fu Chan told me. Father was always so dramatic. His imagination would run wild if we didn't rein him in occasionally."

I jabbed a digit at the photo of the slender man in the robe.

"Can you explain this photo? The one with, I assume, your father and this tall character shaking hands with him?"

Ignored the question, she said: "Would you care for a drink, Mr. Detective? I hear private eyes are hard drinkers."

"Vat 69 if you've got it," I said. "One ice cube. Does that sound like something a private dick would drink? What other rumors have you heard about us seamy detectives?"

She was about as subtle as a runaway boxcar. Without a word, she turned and bent over a low liquor cabinet. From where I sat, the view went all the way to Catalina. This girl had potential, and then some.

"To be completely honest," she continued as she rummaged through the cabinet, "I only know what I've seen in the movies."

She clinked a few bottles to convince me she was still looking.

"In the movies," she explained, "private dicks are a horny bunch of characters. Well, depending on the screenplay I suppose."

"Screenwriters like that get dragged in front of the McCarthy hearings," I replied. "On the whole, we private snoops are an upstanding bunch of n'er-do-wells."

The curtain came down on Catalina when she stood up. She sauntered over with a bottle of Vat 69 and two heavy Mexican water glasses.

"Sorry, I don't have an ice cube," she apologized. "I'll call Mai Ling. She'll bring one."

"That won't be necessary," I said. "I'll take it straight."

She offered me a glass and I took it.

"Say when," she said, and poured enough hooch in my glass to tranquilize a rhino.

"*When* was three fingers ago!" I said. "But we detectives aren't picky."

"Really? May I call you Alex?"

"If that makes you happy."

"Perfect! We're on a first name basis now. Bottoms up?"

"I'll say."

She drank her booze like she wore her skirts, short and fast.

"Now, tell me about this photo," I said, trying to put her train back on track.

"Please, sit down, Alex. We might as well be comfortable while you give me the third degree."

She plopped down on a sofa as long as a California freeway. She was already in the fast lane.

Patting the cushion beside her, she indicated I should sit. I sat, squeezing in between a large pillow and the Dvorak quail's bare thigh.

"Despite what you've seen in the movies," I droned, "I'm not here to give you the third degree. This is just a friendly conversation to help me find out who put the finger on your old man."

"No third degree?" she pouted. "Are you sure? I might like that."

It was getting far too warm in here. I pulled out my pack of Chesterfields, held one out to her.

"Smoke?"

"No, thank you. I don't smoke anything named after furniture. How can you be so sure father's accident was murder?"

"Because..."

And that was as far as I got before she reached across my lap to set her empty glass on the end table next to me. Her breasts brushed against my legs. The scent of lavender infused with sweat filled my head with helium. She couldn't get much closer, but she tried.

"Oh, excuse me," she giggled as she braced her left hand on my thigh. Her body heat creased my pants like a hot iron. In one quick movement, she flipped onto her back and plopped her head on my lap.

This was prom night stuff, but prom night was only a couple of years ago for Isabelle Dvorak, just fun and games. But for a 34-year-old private Richard like me it spelled trouble with a capital T.

"Is this a scene from one of your detective movies?" I laughed. "Or are we just playing house?"

She snaked her arm behind my neck and pulled me close. Her lips burned into mine. They thought they owned me. That's what old money does to a kid. She'd always got whatever she wanted, and this time it was me. The salty taste of her lips made it hard for me to think straight. I slipped my hand under her sweater and found her rich girl breasts. They were firm and sweaty, but they were two speed bumps on the road to catch a killer. I snapped out of my helium high and sat up.

"You still haven't told me about that damn photo," I growled.

"Good Lord!" she gasped. "We're all business now?"

"Your screenplay just got a rewrite, sister. Give."

Sitting up, she pulled her sweater down and adjusted her skirt, what little there was of it.

"All right, yes, that picture was taken at Omenon's Inverness headquarters," she pouted. "The man with the beard is Ananda Vedanta. The occasion was Father's initiation, Halloween night, 1948. There, happy?"

"What gives with your pop and this crazy cult, anyway?" I said, taking a long drag on my smoke. "Why would a Berkeley professor with a stash like this fall for a song and dance like Omenon? Was he a lost soul or did he just like the way he looked in robes?"

"Very funny," she snipped. "Father had a reputation for immersing himself in whatever he was researching, sort of like undercover work. Omenon was his latest project. You do realize he was a world-famous sociologist? He wrote *The Hooked Nose Fetish of the Astrofarian Concubine*, among other major works."

I inhaled my last drop of Vat 69.

"Don't get me started on the Astrofarians," I said. Now that I had put the brakes on Miss Dvorak's libido, she was finally dishing some dirt.

"Go on," I coaxed. "Keep talking."

"Like I said, Omenon was his latest study," the nympho continued. "He was fascinated by sub-groups, you know, cults; how they emerge, grow, and eventually self-destruct. It's how he got first-hand material for his books."

"So, he wasn't a loony cultist himself," I said. "He infiltrated their ranks to find out whatever he needed to find out."

"Yes, that's how it was."

"Well, what did he find out?"

"That, I can't tell you. What I mean to say is, I don't know. Father never confided in me about his work, at least, not until his publisher had his finished manuscript."

"Too bad," I said. "Maybe he learned something. Maybe he learned something that gave someone a reason to send him over a cliff. Thanks for the drink, Miss Dvorak, and for the information."

"So, we're back to Miss Dvorak again. What happened to Belle?"

"Look, you think this is fun and games," I said. "It's not. We already have two murders connected to this case. We need to stay focused. There's a good chance you could be a target yourself. That's why I want you to call me if you ever feel threatened, or if there's anything that seems suspicious to you. Here's my card."

"You do realize I haven't given up on you, Alex. Rrruff!"

9
Roswell Dvorak Speaks

The tower lights on the Golden Gate Bridge flashed their steady warning as I drove toward the city. The waters below the bridge looked as black as a politician's conscience. The sun had set a couple hours ago, so I made haste to my Telegraph Hill apartment stash. Paloma had already let herself in and fallen asleep in the easy chair next to the Philco highboy. She opened her eyes when I came through the front door.

"You smell like day old lavender, detective. Must have been a tough interview."

"She was a scrawny old bird," I said. "A bit of a schoolmarm and not too chatty, but I got some useful tidbits out of her."

"Did someone biff you on the kisser or is that lipstick?"

"She wasn't chatty, more like persistent. In any case, I brought home the bacon."

"How's about we put the bacon under the covers and warm up a late-night snack?" Paloma liked this bacon analogy. She'd used it on me before. Then I noticed her bare skin peeking out from under my robe. She caught me admiring her basic instincts.

"Oh, I suppose you want your robe back, huh?" she toyed. "It's too itchy anyway." She untied the belt, removed the robe.

"Better? No itchy old robe."

Her body glowed in the dim light.

"Okay, big boy," she said. "Let's put a log on the fire and warm things up."

It's moments like this that makes me lose track of time. Before I knew it, the moon slid across Nob Hill all the way to Ocean Beach. My pack of Chesterfields had somehow worked their way down to the foot of the bed. That's where I found them.

I fired one up as I watched Paloma sleeping. This new schedule of hers confused me. Used to be she'd be dancing her feathers off at Andy Wong's every night of the week. Then she changed everything. Now she dances afternoons some days and evenings on others. Then she decided she wanted three full days off every week. Said she needed the time to pursue her new sleuthing career.

But tonight, the floorshow was in my Telegraph Hill apartment. Lying in bed, Paloma's skin glowed like a radium dial on a Timex watch.

I spanked her apple bottom. Like Santa, it jiggled like a bowl full of jelly.

"Hey, Legs! Did you remember to bring the board?"

She snapped out of her dream and growled: "Easy on the moneymaker, barbarian! Of course I brought it. It's over there on the table."

"It's time to contact the egghead again, Kitten. It turns out his troubles began when he joined a kooky cult run by some crackpot named Ananda Vedanta. The Prof's daughter said he was working on a book about the guy's cult when his car careened over the cliff."

Paloma hadn't budged. I walked my fingers along the inside of her thigh. When I reached San Berdoo, she jumped.

"Hey, ya big palooka!" she yelped, and kicked her legs at me.

"Chop chop, Angel Puss. Get with the heavy breathing, and I don't mean the other kind."

Paloma yanked a blanket off the bed to wrap her naked lineaments. We sat in our facing chairs as before, board balanced on our knees. She began breathing deeply, rhythmically. Each time she filled her lungs, the blanket opened slightly, revealing her 34D clockworks in motion.

"Professor Dvorak!" she droned imploringly. "Can you hear me?"

The thingamabob lurched to "YES."

Whispering, I said: "Ask him what the secret word is. I don't want a half-baked highbinder stalking my stash."

"Professor Dvorak," Paloma continued, "can you tell us your secret word?"

The planchette spelled, "MARIN." An avalanche of words then followed. It took time to write it all down. I did the writing on a notepad I'd labeled, "Séances."

"GO TO GIANT CAMERA 3PM TUESDAY MEET MAN IN PANAMA HAT THAT IS ALL."

The only Giant Camera I knew was the tourist attraction by that name stashed behind the Cliff House. It was a small shack built to look like a camera. It could hold, at most, a dozen people inside, huddled around a concave, white dish on the floor. The dish was a viewing screen.

A hollow pyramid with mirrors inside turned round and round on the Giant Camera's roof. The mirrors took in a 360° view of their surroundings, and bounced the images down onto the screen. It was daVinci's *camera obscura*, and just one thin dime got you inside for a look-see.

Maybe this was the break I was looking for.

10
Little Pete's Getting Married

On occasion, the office phone rings. And when it does, Paloma answers it. This time, a woman's voice came through the wire. She sounded young, refined, formal.

The voice said: "May I speak with Alexander Blade, please?"

In an aloof, professional tone, Paloma replied: "Whom shall I say is calling?"

The voice said: "Isabelle Dvorak."

Paloma covered the phone's mouthpiece with her palm.

"Alex, it's the scrawny old bird. Better hurry. She's probably too weak to hold the phone much longer."

"Thanks, I've got it. You can hang up now. Miss Dvorak? What can I do for you?"

Her voice purred like a well-fed ocelot.

"You can start by calling me Belle instead of Miss Dvorak, Alex," she said. "I thought we were friends."

"Isabelle, is there a point to this call, or are we just feeling bored today?"

"You are always in such a snit, Alex. Okay, you told me to call if I felt threatened. Well, I feel threatened."

"In what way?"

"There's been a car parked on the road outside the front gate. It was there when I went to bed last night and it's still there. It's a dark blue sedan with two men wearing dark suits in the front seat. They just sit there smoking and reading newspapers. Mai Ling got the license plate number when she went out to check the mailbox."

"Good job," I said. "Let's have it."

"Late model Chrysler, '48 or '49 with California plates. Got a pencil? STN666."

"Got it. I'll have it traced," I said.

A pause ensued on her end of the line.

"You mean you're not coming over to protect me?"

"I've got an appointment. But I'll be in touch as soon as I find out who owns that Chrysler. Just stay put and keep the doors locked."

"You're no fun," she pouted, and rang off.

Paloma hadn't hung up her end of the phone as instructed. She'd laid the receiver on her desk within earshot.

"No lavender-laced hankies today?" she quipped.

"I won't dignify that comment with a response."

I opened my address book to R and dialed Stan Raycraft's desk at the *Call-Bulletin*. Stan had run plates for me before, using his DMV contact. He was guzzling a glass of mulled wine when he picked up. A radio blaring holiday tunes tempered the clash of typewriter keys banging out the late edition.

"Hi dee ho and gadzooks," he slurred. "It's your favorite reporter, Stanley Raycraft, Esquire, at your service. To whom am I speaking?"

"Stan! This is Blade. I'm in a jam. It's too complicated to explain the gory details, especially since you're as drunk as a fiddler's witch. You wouldn't believe me anyway."

"It's Christmas, Buster! I'll believe anything! And I've been a very good boy this year."

"Stan, listen. I have a favor to ask. It's important. Two no-goodniks in a Chrysler are stalking a helpless young lady's wikiup. You could save this nice girl a lot of grief if you'd track down the owner of that car. It'll put you in solid with Mrs. Claus, too."

"Buster, if I can help a babe in distress, I'm all over it. What's the plate number? We'll show 'em. While you're at it, give me the babe's number too."

"We'll talk about that later. Got a pencil? It's California plate STN666."

"Ho ho! That's a good one. I'll get back to you toot sweet with the dope, pal."

I quaffed two coffin nails and a slug of Vat 69 waiting for Stan's return call. I snatched up the phone on the first ring. He was even more plastered than the last time we talked.

He slurred: "I come bearing great and glorious g-gifts from the city by the b-bay, Buzzter. But I must s-say, you've piqued my reporter's curiosity, Big Daddy. What's got your knickers in a twist? What gives with the sinister stalkers and the cute girlie?"

"I'll be happy to sit down with you and give you the big scoop, but right now I need that info, Stan!"

"Okay, okay. Juz don't forget old Stanley when you close in for the pinch, hokay? The car's registered to a Hector Skelter, 13 Mt. Vision Road, Inverness. That's California, not Scotland. Hic.

"Say, Buzzter, did you know that's the world headquarters for Omenum, Omen-a, whatever, a gloom 'n doom cult for schizos and

Stan Raycraft

dipsos? Hector Skelter is their guru's muscle. He's a honcho in the Galactic Rangers, or whatever his boss man calls 'em.

"Buster, I kid you not," Stan rambled. "This Ananda Vedanta guru dude is one mean cat. He's about ten feet tall, never cuts his hair, has looong chin whiskers down to his ankles, wears a loooong flooowing robe, and no shoes. Not even socks. Can you believe it? But he's jake with the goofball politicians and bleeding hearts who think he does wunnerful work keeping boozers 'n junkies off the streets. The Chrysler outside your lady friend's house is jus' one of a fleet registered to that same address."

I promised Stan I'd meet him at Tommy's Place when the coast was clear to give him the full story. I'd no sooner hung up the phone when the scent of sandalwood filled the office.

"Have you been burning incense, Legs?"

"Not me, but I smell it, too," she said.

The TV set surged. A sulfurous cloud rose from its electronic innards. The 12-inch picture tube glowed red, as an image of Fung Jing Toy slowly came into focus.

"Greetings, Kum How," his electronic tonsils quavered. "So nice to see your radiant face again."

The slant-eyed scoundrel was looking straight at Paloma.

"Are you talking to me?" Paloma asked.

"Of course," the highbinder leered. "We have many moons of unfinished business to attend to, from a time when you were the most coveted girl in Chinatown. You were my Golden Peach, loved by many, but none more than myself. I was about to take you to China as my bride when my unworthy opponents had me killed. I have been searching for you ever since."

Paloma protested. "Look, whoever you think I am, and whatever you say I was in the good old days, has nothing to do with me now. I'm a bebop chick from the Atomic Age, and you're a fuzzy hatchet handler inside a TV tube."

"Now as then," the specter sputtered, "things can be arranged. You have paid my debt to the Lord of the Underworld, and I am free to make our wedding arrangements."

"Hold on, highbinder," I squawked, "I've got two cents to add to this gab fest. You're harassing my lovely assistant. The lady said no, so hoist your pigtail and blow."

"This blue-eyed devil will be taught to respect his elders, Kum How," the spirit in the TV snarled. "We shall discuss our wedding at a later time, when we are alone. Meanwhile, my Golden Peach, pack your trousseau." The television flickered a few times before it blacked out.

I frowned at Paloma. "So, weejee boards are a piece of cake, right? It'll be a lead pipe cinch. Looks to me like you're first in line to become Mrs. Little Pete."

"That board is getting on my nerves," Paloma shivered. "We've got to do something before that tintype Romeo comes back. He thinks I'm this Kum How person he used to know."

"Drastic situations call for drastic measures," I said. "Coming from me, I know this sounds crazy, but we've got to talk to Berkeley Livingstone."

"Ask him about the Chief," Paloma advised. "Livingstone says the Chief's got what it takes."

11
Strawberry Hill

We screeched to a stop in front of the Metaphysical Bookstore. At that very moment, Berkeley Livingstone was taping a flyer to an A-frame signboard in front of the shop. He had placed the sign in the middle of the sidewalk so pedestrians had to walk around it; the point being, they would assume it was something important, like "watch out for falling objects," or "don't touch the live wires," ergo, they would read it. The flyer said: "Come to Séance Sunday! Meet The Chief! Amazing insights! Astounding revelations! Free popcorn!"

"Hey there, Berk! The Chief is just the guy we want to see," I quacked as we closed in on the disheveled book bender. I often wondered if Livingstone owned just one set of clothes or several identical outfits. Either way, he always looked the same—baggy gray trousers, light blue pinstriped shirt without a collar, brown suspenders, and leather sandals over dingy white socks.

"Sorry, Buster. You're too early to see the Chief," Livingstone yeeped. "He won't be here until Sunday. Why, hello, Miss Paloma. Did you enjoy your book on Ouija boards?"

"It opened doors I'd rather keep shut," she replied. "We've got to talk to the Chief, Mr. Livingstone. We're in trouble with an evil spirit in our board."

"I see. Well, this isn't the first time I've heard about a talking board that made trouble. I have a few books dealing with this kind of attack, but I recommend the 1930 edition of Dion Fortune's *Psychic Self Defense*. It has a well-rounded approach."

Livingstone's chatter began to annoy me.

"Listen, Berk, we're past the do-it-yourself stuff." I barked. "We need an expert. We've got to see the Chief, the real deal, and I mean now."

"I'm afraid Chief Iron Lung has no phone. For that matter, he has no address, either. As I recall, he said he'd pitched his teepee in Golden Gate Park somewhere. Where was it? He doesn't go in for big city living, you see. He's like an island unto himself.

"Yes, that's it! He's camped on an island called Strawberry Hill in Stow Lake. I'm sure you know it. You can rent small boats there. He doesn't usually leave the island until three or four in the afternoon, so I expect he's there now."

"Thanks, Berk, gotta run," I yeeped as we dashed back to the Hudson.

Time was of the essence. Little Pete could reappear any minute to drool over his Golden Peach. We still couldn't figure how Pete thought he'd pull off his marriage, what with Paloma being flesh and blood, and Pete being a fuzzy picture inside a TV set. But we weren't going to wait around to sort it all out.

I white-knuckled the Hudson down Geary, hung a left on two wheels at Park Presidio, and reached Golden Gate Park in record time. Crossover Road took us straight to the Stow Lake boathouse, where we parked the car and hightailed it to the lake. We could have rented a boat to putt-putt our way to Strawberry Hill, but we were in a hurry, so, we used the stone bridge.

It turned out Strawberry Hill was a steep climb, nearly 400 feet. The trail petered out at the old observatory ruins. In its heyday, the steel and concrete observatory was a destination for tourists who came for impressive park views. But the '06 quake destroyed the building and it was never replaced. It's been a picturesque ruin ever since.

Livingstone said the Chief's camp was somewhere near the ruin. A wisp of smoke in the distance gave us a clue. We followed a vague path through coyote brush and pine trees until we lamped an unusual sight, even for Golden Gate Park: a teepee painted with mystical symbols pitched in a clearing. In front of the teepee, a man sat cross-legged warming himself next to a campfire. The campsite was above Huntington Falls, an artificial waterfall. Water gushed down the falls and was pulled back up with an electric pump. The campfire was real, though. It smoldered and popped under a beat-up tin coffee pot.

I'd read enough Zane Grey novels to know this had to be the Chief. He sat as still as a loaf of bread contemplating who-knows-what as smoke rose from a hand-rolled coffin nail in his kisser. He wore a red cotton shirt with white polka dots, tanned deerskin pants with leather fringe down the sides, a blue 'kerchief strung around his neck, and a weathered top hat with an eagle feather stuck in the band.

Somehow, he knew we were coming before we got within sighting distance. We could hear him chanting:

"Fee fum foe fye, I smell the blood of white eye."

We approached him and for a moment we just stood there, not knowing what to say. So, the Indian spoke first.

"Okay, why white man seek the Chief, as if he didn't know?"

"Chief, my name is Alexander Blade, and this is my assistant, Paloma Liu Tsong. Berkeley Livingstone said we'd find you here. We've got a serious problem we hope you can help us solve."

"Humpf," the Chief said as he puffed his wheezer. "White eye jump into hot water with no life jacket, huh?"

"You have a way with words, Chief. That about sums it up."

Paloma began to speak, but Iron Lung cut her off.

"No need for yellow squaw to say," he said. "Let Chief guess. You have evil spirit on loose due to mishap with talking board. Correct?"

Paloma's eyes couldn't have gotten wider. She replied:

"Why, y-yes, that's right!"

"And you want Joe Iron Lung to dispose of bad spirit."

"Correct again, Chief," I dittoed. "How about it?"

"Sorry, Chief got busy schedule."

"Busy?!" I yeeped. "Busy doing what?"

Chief Joe Iron Lung

"Hunting White Lady in Lake," he replied. "Waters around this island haunted, big time. Writing book about it: *In Search of White Lady in Lake*, by Chief Iron Lung."

I had heard of this White Lady in the Lake, but assumed it was an urban legend. I said:

"Is this the white lady who lost her baby in the lake 50 years ago?"

"Same," the Chief said, blowing smoke rings above his head.

"The same white lady that scares boaters when she floats up out of the water and asks them if they've seen her baby?"

"You catch on fast for white eye," the Chief said.

Paloma, being hip to this kind of thing, jumped in.

"I know how to find White Lady in the Lake, Chief," she said excitedly. "My cousin told me how to call her. All you have to do is take your canoe out on the lake. When you reach the Chinese pagoda on the shore, chant: 'White Lady, White Lady, I have your baby,' three times. White Lady will rise out of the lake and ask, 'Have you seen my baby?' If you say yes, she'll haunt you. If you say no, she'll kill you. It's one of those "lose-lose' hauntings."

"Chief hear that one before," he replied. "Chief has own system. Just takes time."

"Listen, Chief," I persisted, "White Lady has been haunting this lake for 50 years, right?"

"Chief not add up total, but close enough."

"Well, our evil spirit is a sure thing, and it's urgent. It's running amok in my office, a real nuisance. I'd be willing to pay a hefty chunk of change if you'd get rid of it."

"I see," said the Chief. "White eye speaks language of dead presidents now. In that case, Chief's evil spirit exorcism package start at 100 dead presidents. For you, Chief put White Lady on back burner. First, we take Chief's equipment to job site. You got metal wagon that travel without horse?"

"If you mean a car, yes, it's parked at the boathouse," I replied. "We'll even help you pack."

Between the three of us, we carried four heavy canvas sacks of the Chief's exorcism gear down Strawberry Hill to my heap. The trunk on a Hudson coupe is as deep as the Grand Canyon, so the Chief's drums, headdresses, smudge pots, herbs, beaded vestments, bells, magical sticks, and amulets all fit inside. I slammed the lid shut, and we were off, heckity blip, to the Mayfair Building.

12

The Chief vs. Little Pete

Little Pete was waiting for us when we arrived. The Admiral's picture tube had that astral red glow, as it did whenever Pete was the featured bozo. He spoke only when Paloma entered the room.

"How is my lotus flower today?" he smirked. "I trust you have been packing for our glorious voyage back to China."

I led the Chief to the TV.

"Chief, meet Little Pete," I said.

The Chief glared at the glowing cathode ray tube. His weathered mug wrinkled in a perplexed frown.

"Why evil spirit in box with big red eye?"

Then it hit me. The Chief was clueless about post-war electronic gadgets. Having lived in an isolated village up north until a few weeks ago, he had never witnessed the miracle of television.

I explained: "You know what radio is, right, Chief?"

"You bet. The Shadow, Fibber McGee, Nick Carter Private Eye."

"Correct right down the line, Chief. TV is like radio, but with moving pictures, sound with pictures. The evil spirit somehow got out of his talking board and moved into this talking picture box. See?"

"Okay, no big deal," the Chief replied. "I got system. Fix in no time."

"I beg to differ, red man," the sinister voice within the box said. It made crackling, squealing sounds the Chief had never heard before.

From out of nowhere a hatchet zipped within inches of Iron Lung's kisser. It buried itself in a wall after slicing off the front of his hat brim. The Chief took out a handkerchief and blew his hooked trumpet. He did not seem perturbed.

"Spirit toss a mean tomahawk," he observed. "Better get to work, before aim get better."

The shaman began moving chairs around. He pushed Paloma's desk out of the way, closed the Venetian blinds, and replaced his damaged top hat with a feathered headdress. Reaching into a deerskin sack, he pulled out a bundle of white sage and placed it in a clay pot. Striking a flint on a small stone, he made a spark. The sage caught the spark, and thick, aromatic smoke filled the room.

"Evil spirits hate this stuff," the Chief explained.

"It's not doing wonders for me either, Chief," I wheezed. "Tell you what, we'll leave you to your work. I've got a case that should keep me out of the office for quite a while. And I'd prefer it if Paloma stayed away while you take care of you-know-who in the picture box."

The Chief replied: "Chief make self at home. Where cook stove?"

"No kitchen, Chief," Paloma said as she reached into her desk drawer. "Here's a roll of dimes. There's a snack dispenser down the hall. It's not much, but it's all we've got."

"Machine that give out snacks? White eyes sure come up with crazy stuff. However, Chief expect to dine on swell Oriental cuisine at dinnertime. Put on expense account."

"What expense account?" I choked. "You never mentioned expenses!"

"Chief forgot. Not to worry. Chief take care of evil spirit."

"If you see any bats," Paloma said, "take care of those, too."

"No problem. Spirit rodents just tiny extra fee."

13
The Giant Camera

The Giant Camera hugged the edge of a rocky cliff overlooking the blue Pacific Ocean and an even bluer December sky. I was loitering behind the Cliff House on a wide, concrete veranda. I waited there about five minutes, long enough to crush a gasper under the toe of my brogan.

I watched families playing tag with the waves on Ocean Beach below. Even at this time of year tourists get a crazy idea to don swimsuits and jump into the freezing water so they can send snapshots to envious neighbors back home, wherever there's snow this time of year.

I pulled my coat sleeve up and checked my strap watch. It was three o'clock on the nose, so I strolled to the Giant Camera's ticket booth to roust the bearded Bohemian behind the window. He put down his copy of *Planet Stories* long enough to take my dime and wave me through.

I pushed aside the swing doors and entered. Total darkness blinded me at first. Aside from the faint whirring of an electric motor somewhere in the ceiling, the room was as quiet as the library reading room. A slow-moving image of Ocean Beach appeared on the floor screen behind a metal railing. I saw waves sparkle in the winter sun. Tiny spots moving to and fro on the beach were people.

As my eyes became accustomed to the dark, I saw a man on the other side of the room. What caught my eye was the Panama hat he wore. Not counting the bearded geezer out front, we were the only two stiffs in the camera.

This had to be the guy the board was talking about. But it didn't tell me about a secret handshake or whatever it was I needed to confirm my contact. So, I improvised.

"Would you be a friend of Dr. Roswell Dvorak?" I blurted at the dark figure.

The Panama hat turned in my direction. It was still too dark to make out a face.

"And who might you be?" the figure replied.

"The name is Alexander Blade. Fu Chan hired me. Like I said, do you know Roswell Dvorak?"

"I should. I am Dvorak."

"What? You? Dvorak?" I sputtered. "Maybe you haven't read the papers, pal. Dvorak is dead."

"I tell you I'm Roswell Dvorak!" the figure persisted. "The body in my car belonged to a hitchhiker I'd picked up in Half Moon Bay. I escaped at the last minute, before the car went over the cliff. My passenger wasn't so lucky. He was asleep. I yelled, but it was too late."

"Why the disappearing act?" I pressed. "And what's with the cloak and dagger weejee board baloney?"

"Can we go somewhere less public? This will take time to explain," he said.

"Sutro Heights Park is up the street," I said. "It's nearly Christmas. We should have it all to ourselves. We can talk there."

Exiting the Giant Camera into the afternoon sun, I finally got a gander at the formerly deceased sociologist. Besides the Panama, he wore a blue plaid gabardine coat, a bright yellow shirt, white cotton pants, no vest, and no tie. His outfit was strictly off-season, especially the hat. We walked in silence past the Cliff House gift shops and the Sutro baths, up the long, steep sidewalk that followed Pt. Lobos Street.

At the corner of 48th and Pt. Lobos we entered the park, passing a brace of lifelike stone lions reclining on massive concrete pedestals. Once upon a time, these lions watched over the estate of Gold Rush millionaire Adolph Sutro. His mansion was abandoned after his death, and it burned to the ground during the Depression. Then the city took over fashioned the property into a public park.

I scanned our surroundings. We were alone, except for an elderly couple exploring the gardens. The woman wore a fur coat that dated her age and a hat fashioned from last year's pheasant hunt. She took photos of the Cliff House far below.

Strolling through the well-manicured gardens, we found a wood bench with a million-dollar view. To our left, the Great Highway cut through the dunes like a long, gray scar. Ahead of us, the Pacific Ocean loomed vast and deep. A stone parapet ringed the edge of the cliff where we sat. The view was all that remained of Sutro's fabulous seaside estate, but it was still a doozey.

After setting fire to a Chesterfield, I said: "Before we get started, let's see some ID. Under the circumstances, I think you understand."

He pulled a worn lizard skin wallet from an inside coat pocket, showed me a California driver license, a UC Berkeley faculty card, a Bancroft Library card, and a university cafeteria card, all with his name on them. The cafeteria card had three punch holes in it: Monday, Wednesday, and Friday. No doubt about it, the natty dresser sitting next to me was Dr. Roswell Dvorak.

"Now that you know who I am, may I see your ID, Mr. Blade?"

I obliged him with a swivel of my PI's license and my official-looking gold buzzer. He seemed satisfied enough to spill the beans.

"After I've told you my story, I'm sure you'll appreciate the secrecy I've had to live with since the accident," the Professor explained. "Not even my daughter, Isabelle, knows I'm alive. I can only imagine how difficult this has been for her."

"She looked devastated a few days ago, but she's soldiering on," I embellished.

"I'm afraid it was necessary," Dvorak frowned. "I suppose you know that I'm a sociologist. For several years my research has focused on marginalized groups controlled by charismatic leaders. They call often themselves prophets, but society generally views these groups as cults. Such cults coalesce around psychic revelations, political ideologies, even taboo sexual practices. Some cults have all three. But one factor remains the same; the cult must have a prophet."

"Your daughter told me you were studying Omenon from the inside."

"My approach is unconventional compared to my peers. I create a fabricated identity and embed myself within the group. With my knowledge of the inner workings of such cults, I know exactly how to approach them. So, last year I joined Omenon as a repentant alcoholic, using the name, Lester Brannon.

"I showed them some of my writing, done not by Roswell Dvorak but by my new persona. They put me to work in the Omenon archive, tasked with the job of ghostwriting Ananda Vedanta's upcoming autobiography, *The Naked and the Nuked: A Prophet for the Atomic Age.*

"What I discovered during my research was far more insidious than the average cult, if there is such a thing as an average cult. What I learned made me realize I could not continue my charade without dire consequences to the world and to my personal safety.

"So, I gave an excuse for returning to life as a 'Norm' and withdrew my membership. A Norm is what Vedanta calls outsiders who don't belong to Omenon. He also has a word for anyone who leaves the group for any reason. Pharisees, he calls them. But leaving the group was as dangerous as staying in; maybe worse. Mr. Blade, the steering gear on my car completely disconnected before it went over that cliff. It was no accident.

"The newspapers said my automobile was so badly damaged the actual cause of the accident couldn't be determined. The police assumed the charred body in the wreckage was mine, which was a fortuitous error on their part. I could then disappear and no one would look for me. I flagged a ride from a passing motorist who dropped me at a bus stop in Linda Mar. From there, I made my way back to San Francisco by bus. Believe me, Mr. Blade, if Ananda Vedanta knew he'd failed to kill me, I'd still be in his crosshairs."

"I see your point," I said. "Where've you been hiding all this time?"

"I knew of an abandoned caretaker's cottage behind one of the windmills in Golden Gate Park. The windmills haven't been used in years, and the cottage had everything I needed to stay out of sight, except food, of course. I've been living on midway food from the Playland amusement park nearby, where I'm just one of the crowd. If I ever get out of this mess, I'll never eat another corn dog as long as I live!"

"That's understandable," I said. "But how'd you get the basic necessities of life, like folding dough, toothpaste and such?"

"Fu Chan was the only person that knew I was still alive. He helped me survive. When I returned to San Francisco after the accident, I swore him to secrecy. We wrote that letter and locked it in my desk drawer, making it seem like it had been there all along. But Fu Chan didn't tell you that we engaged the services of a native shaman I know. I made it worth his while to come to San Francisco and work with Fu Chan.

"He sent those Ouija board messages via the etheric plane. He does this while in a trance brought on by the sacred peyote plant. It's truly amazing. When he isn't sending messages to you, he's lecturing on the ritual use of peyote at the Metaphysical bookstore. His name is Joseph Iron Lung."

"You mean the Chief? Why, that two-timing pipsqueak."

"You know him?"

"You bet I do. He's in my office right now, exorcising trouble that came through that talking board Fu Chan gave us. The Chief acted like he had all this mystical foreknowledge about our weejee board troubles before we even asked for his help. What a shyster!"

"Well, if anyone can help you, it's Chief Iron Lung. I've learned to respect the transcendental abilities of native shamans. The Chief knew exactly how to send and receive messages through the board in your office. Obviously, it worked. That was our plan and now you're here."

"I don't get it," I spat. "Why all the smoke and mirrors? Fu Chan could have slipped me a note and cut out the Chief and the weejee board entirely."

"True, my plan was complicated, but, other than my 'last request' letter, it left no paper trail," Dvorak explained. "Blame it on Omenon, Mr. Blade. It uses Ouija boards as part of its brainwashing technique. The one Fu Chan gave you was my personal Omenon board. Every member receives one as part of his initiation into the Teachings."

I pulled up my collar as an offshore breeze crept down my neck.

"I'm going to take you to my apartment where I can keep an eye on you," I said. "It's nowhere near as luxurious as your Marin County digs, but it's got more creature comforts than that caretaker's cottage of yours. If you have back there you want to bring with you, you should get it."

"There's nothing there that I want, but I should clear it out as a safety precaution. I'll need some new toiletries and such once I get re-settled."

I checked our surroundings. The sightseeing couple in the garden had long since disappeared. My car was far below Sutro Heights, parked at the Cliff House. We walked down Pt. Lobos, reaching the Hudson in far less time than it took to get to the park.

Back on Telegraph Hill, I reorganized my apartment stash for my new roommate. Dvorak took a shower and borrowed some duds from my clothes closet. They almost fit, just a little extra room thanks to my extra heft. With the Professor safely tucked away, I drove back to the office to check in on the Chief.

14
The Mind Fuhrer

If someone had told me last week that an Indian chief was in my office smoking jimson weed and pounding a tom tom twelve hours a day, I'd have told them they were nuts. Shows you what I know. Not only was there a chief in my office, he was charging me a hundred bucks to keep him there.

According to my strap watch, I'd given the Chief a full six hours to get rid of the highbinder. I was ready for the gory details.

Paloma's sleigh bells jingled on the door as I entered the office. I yanked them off.

"Bah! Humbug," I growled. "How'd it go, Chief? Is Little Pete playing Mah Jong with his highbinder pals back in China?"

"Phooey," the Chief spat.

"He's gone, right?"

"Here we go again," droned the Chief. "White eye capitalist puppet want everything pronto, chop chop, big rush. White eye big dope when it come to spirit world. Time not exist in spirit world, see? Could be now, could be later. By the way, Chief is tuckered out from drumming all day. What 'bout dinner?"

As my mush curdled listening to the Chief's song and dance, Paloma was at the Sky Room in her nude thong flapping two feathered fans to a live jazz combo. Now and then she'd lift the fans to give the crowd a glimpse of the bountiful melon patch behind the feathered curtain. That always brought down the house.

Nearing the end of her routine, she piped an odd-looking mug in the first row. He wasn't there a minute ago, she thought, and he didn't have that goofy pie-eyed look of the average tourist. His face twisted and writhed like a piece of wet leather on a bed of hot coals. Fung Jing Toy!

Paloma raised her fans high above her head, gave the cheering crowd its money's worth, and cut the act short. As the curtain fell, she made a beeline to the nearest phone and dialed our office. I picked up.

"Alex, L-Little P-Pete is here in the Sky Room!" she shuddered. "He's in the first row, and his aura is full of creepy vibrations. I'm getting out of here."

"Hold on, Legs! Let me ask the Chief what gives."

I laid the dilemma on Iron Lung, who gave his usual matter-of-fact explanation.

"It only seem like Little Pete in Sky Room," the Chief explained. "Will take another full moon before Pete manifest in flesh body. Okay, Chief change gears. Bring in heavy artillery. Meantime, invite beautiful China princess to dinner with us."

I took my palm off the receiver. "Legs? Can you meet us at Sam Woo's for dinner? Just come as you are, Kitten." The line clicked off on her end.

Twenty minutes and two orders of spring rolls later, I lamped Paloma, hefting her weary gams onto the top stair of Sam Woo's third floor dining room. She had an escort. Stan Raycraft, hotshot reporter and gourmet firewater guzzler at the Call-Bulletin was hooked to her arm.

"I see you ran into trouble on the way over," I said to Paloma as they plopped down on two empty chairs.

Stan feigned hurt feelings at my remark.

"Hey, not so, Big Daddy. This beautiful lady invited me to the party. Well, maybe I twisted her arm to let me tag along. What's up, my man?"

"The rent, and it ain't been paid."

"Whatever you say Buster, but don't forget, I've got a nose for news, and right now my nose is twitching."

"Okay, Stan," I said. "Tell me all you know about that guru head honcho of the Omenon church."

Raycraft's eyebrows arched like two wooly question marks. "You mean the Mind Fuhrer?" he gulped. "That's what his followers call him. If you've got business with that cat, you've got trouble."

"Jesus breezes!" Paloma snapped. "Doesn't anybody want to hear what happened to me at the club today? My ticket to China nearly got punched. Chief, you said Pete was under control. How did his ugly mug get into the front row at my performance?"

The Chief shrugged his bony shoulders. "Chief's incantation chased him out of office as planned. Thought he'd be goner by now. Not to worry. Chief send cosmic dragnet. Bring back dead or deader."

"Pete keeps calling me Kum How," she went on. "I'm his Golden Peach, he says. What's he talking about?"

"Kum How?" Stan bleated, "Golden Peach? Well, hot damn!"

Stan was a history buff from way back, and Chinatown was his specialty.

"Kum How was only the most sought-after working girl in Chinatown before the Big Quake," Stan enthused. "I wrote a story about Kum How and Little Pete. He had the hots for her in a big way. She worked out of a brothel in Ross Alley and was Little Pete's favorite. But Junior Boy Chang fawned over her too. Pete and Junior Boy got into a nasty vendetta. Their tongs were at perpetual war, mostly over Kum How. It turned into a big problem for the Chinatown Squad. It spent all its time as the referee for these two warring tongs.

"That is, until Junior Boy got serious. He hired two out-of-town Chinese gunsels to beef Little Pete, which wasn't an easy gig. Pete had a white bodyguard. That was real clever on Pete's part because it was taboo for any Chinese to kill a white man. Pete wore chain mail, too, and a metal bowl inside his hat. He carried a revolver, a hatchet, and an eight-inch knife on his person at all times. That meant the killers had to resort to stealth.

"They knew they'd find him every third Thursday at a Chinese barbershop on Washington Street, where he got a shave and shampoo. Pete's white bodyguard stood outside the front door to make sure no one came in or out without him knowing about it. The gunsels lured the bodyguard from his post just long enough to get inside and shove a revolver up Pete's chain mail underwear. No more Little Pete. His last words were, 'Kum ... How.'"

Stan turned to Paloma. "That was 1897. What's it got to do with you?"

Paloma groaned. "I had a feeling there was more to this. You might as well know, Stan. Little Pete is back in Chinatown, thanks to me. First, he spoke to us through a weejee board. Then I paid his debt to the Underworld, not knowing it was Pete. Now he says I'm his Golden Peach and we're getting married. He wants to take me to China."

"Holy rice cakes!" Stan squawked. "This is like that Boris Karloff movie where he's a mummy. He comes back to reclaim his sexy, reincarnated girlfriend. I need to spend more time in your office! You guys are into some wild stuff, man! I can dig it!"

"We'll be adding a cover charge soon," I said. "We'll wave yours if you help us with some scuttlebutt on Vedanta."

Stan looked nervous. "Hey, my knees are knocking already, man. Where the Mind Fuhrer goes, I do not. Sir Francis Drake highway is the only way into Inverness and the only way out. That makes it easy for Vedanta to keep track of who comes and goes.

"He's got the area staked out with his personal storm troop called the Galactic Rangers. They keep the locals scared stiff, so they stay away from Vedanta's turf. The Galactic Rangers keep tabs on everybody's business over there."

Stan's story got even stranger. Vedanta's real name was Franticek Drtikol, a former science fiction writer. He had some sort of revelation in the desert, brought on by an alien presence. This so-called alien told him to write a series of science fiction yarns as the basis for a new world order. When he founded Omenon, Drtikol changed his name to Ananda Vedanta. After that, he stopped shaving, cutting his hair, and wearing shoes.

Stan continued: "Scuttlebutt says Vedanta's inner circle is full of ex-Nazis straight out of Hitlertown. And there's something else. When Vedanta bought the Inverness property, he also purchased five acres along Old Lighthouse Road. There's an abandoned cemetery on that land where the Coast Guard used to bury unidentified shipwreck victims. But don't bring any flowers there, Buster, you might end up with a plot of your own. Vedanta has that place buttoned up tight. Members only."

"Have you heard what goes on there?" I asked.

"The ranchers are too scared to talk to reporters," Stan explained. "They're afraid of reprisals from the Mind Fuhrer. But one rancher did tell me he's seen lights moving in that cemetery after dark, with Omenon vehicles coming and going at odd hours."

At that, we folded our chopsticks and parted ways. The Chief walked up Washington Street to the office. Stan caught a taxi to the *Call-Bulletin*, and I walked Paloma to her apartment on Jackson. After saying our goodbyes on the sidewalk—her Chinese landlady gets hot under the collar if guys try to sneak into her girls' apartments—I drove back to Telegraph Hill to check on my client.

15
The Guru

The Professor had settled comfortably into my Telegraph Hill digs. However, he had drawn up a list of items that would make his life even more comfortable. You know how eggheads are.

So, the next day, Paloma took his list to a North Beach smoke shop on Vallejo Street where she bought a Kaywoodie Silhouette to replace the pipe that went over the cliff with the Prof's car. There were only a few days left before Christmas and the smoke shop was throwing a blowout sale. Also on the Prof's list were a tin of Half and Half pipe tobacco, and a set of duds that fit him better than mine.

Professor Roswell Dvorak

I'd moved Confidential Investigations out of our Bush Street office due to the Chief's incessant drumming, making my Telegraph Hill apartment our temporary headquarters. With the Prof settled in, I determined to find out how his name ended up on Vedanta's hit list. A cup of espresso, a biscotti, and a pinch of pipe tobacco smoldering in his Kaywoodie was enough to put the Prof in a chatty mood.

"The fact is," he began between heady puffs on his new briar, "little is known about Franticek Drtikol before 1938. That was his true name, you know. As the story goes, his family came from eastern European aristocracy. They invested heavily in the American stock market, and lost everything in the crash of 1929. After the Drtikols sold the family estate, they went their separate ways to various parts of Europe.

"Franticek's first known public appearance was in 1939, at one of Hitler's Aryan Art exhibits in Berlin. He'd made contacts within the Nazi hierarchy as an art dealer and casual writer of fiction. On rare occasions he freelanced for Joseph Goebbels, writing propaganda for the ministry. But he always knew his true calling was science fiction.

"In truth, Drtikol's loyalty extended no farther than himself. When the war turned against the Nazis, he declared himself a citizen of the world. He boarded a plane for California as the Reich collapsed in 1945. All he brought with him was a suitcase and a desire to become a famous science fiction writer. This is where his story takes a sinister turn. Something happened to him in California. Some say it was a religious experience brought on by a supernatural presence."

"I'll bet." I scoffed.

"Understand that Vedanta is an unrepentant megalomaniac," the Prof cautioned. "And, like others of his kind, he believes his life and achievements are legendary. That is why I as given the task of gathering material for his biography. To place him on the pedestal of immortality."

"This is pretty hard to swallow, Professor," I interrupted. "Drtikol was a mediocre science fiction writer at best. I've read his stories. Every pulp magazine in the states banned his tripe, thanks to pressure from readers."

"I admit, it sounds farfetched, but it's true. We live in a new age that resembles science fiction more than our so-called reality. Fantasy is transformed to fact overnight. Some of the most unlikely and unsavory characters of our time have become influential leaders. That's why I wanted to get on the inside of the Omenon cult. The inner workings of such an organization would be of great value to the academic community."

I filled my lungs with nicotine and exhaled thoughtfully. "Like I said, all I know about this guy is his pulp fiction. His magnum opus was the 'Quo Valis' trilogy."

"Yes, that was the blueprint for his Omenon dogma," the Professor agreed. "Which brings me to the reason I've become a marked man. I believe that's what you wanted to know."

"I'm all ears, Professor."

"While researching Vedanta's biography, I came across some snapshots taken in deepest, darkest Nazi Germany during the war. I saw Drtikol in those photos among a group of Nazi scientists working on a top-secret weapon at the end of the war.

"As the Soviets closed in on Berlin, a German physicist named Odvig Varstag came to the attention of the Soviet government. He was about to be arrested by Russian agents when Drtikol miraculously plucked him from their grasp. Drtikol acquired forged papers for Varstag under the name Regis Toomey. Varstag, or rather Toomey, escaped to Lisbon with this new identity.

"Drtikol became Toomey's sponsor and eventually brought him to California. He's done this for several other Nazis. After founding Omenon, Drtikol made Regis Toomey his Chief Science officer."

I crushed a Chesterfield in the ash stand and fired up a fresh one.

"So, Drtikol is running an underground railroad for ex-Nazis, eh?" I said. "Not much news there, Professor. Uncle Sam has been bringing Nazis here by the boatload. They work for our side now. Werner von Braun was an SS officer until we put him in charge of our new space program. Drtikol must be scooping up Nazis who'd rather not work for the Soviets or Uncle Sam. The ones who'd just as soon swap one fascist nut case for another."

Paloma emerged from the kitchen with a fresh pot of coffee, having overheard the end of Dvorak's monologue.

"Color me clueless," Paloma said, "but why would Ananda Vedanta need a Chief Science Officer?"

"That's an excellent question, Miss Liu, which brings me to the point of my long-winded tale," smiled the Professor. "Two months ago, I was in the Omenon archive working quite late. It had been a long day. As I often did, I went outside, behind the Mt. Vision bunker, for a breath of fresh air. The air is quite invigorating up there. Most enjoyable.

"Well, that's when I overheard Vedanta and Toomey, or rather, Herr Varstag, talking. They're both heavy smokers, and were taking a smoke break. The Omenon bunker sits on an isolated ranch on Mt. Vision Road. It's so quiet up there you can hear the stars twinkle. They had no idea I was sitting behind the trunk of a coastal oak. Varstag was informing Vedanta of his progress on a miniaturized atomic weapon. Several of them, in fact."

Paloma interrupted. "Don't you need plutonium for that? How would these guys have plutonium?"

Dvorak tapped his pipe on the ash stand.

"Believe it or not, some of Vedanta's followers are respected government researchers. In fact, some are in a position to access nuclear materials. Somehow, they've been moving small amounts of plutonium to Omenon. But it's far too dangerous to have radioactive material lying around. I can't imagine where Vedanta keeps it. As to the purpose behind his scheme, a thorough reading of 'Quo Valis' may offer a clue."

I lurched out of my chair to the bookshelves where I kept my magazine collection.

"It just so happens Professor, I have a complete set of *Stupendous Stories*. If I remember right, the first installment of 'Quo Valis' was in the March, 1946 issue."

16

"QUO VALIS"
By Franticek Drtikol

(Chapter 9)
I WAS A DEADBEAT FROM
ANOTHER DIMENSION!

When Klaus Deerhoven pulled the lever to activate Project Mind Fuhrer's Sun Bomb, something went terribly wrong. He and his fellow Nazi scientists had hoped the outcome would be a total annihilation of the advancing Allied forces. Instead, deep within their secret underground vault, they began to shimmer like a heat mirage in the Sahara Desert.

Fear gripped Deerhoven's team as they watched laboratory furniture crumble into atoms until there was no floor to crumble onto. Finally, there was no Deerhoven. More or less. He found himself floating among the flotsam of outer space, where stars shone like bits of chromium against the backdrop of eternity. The planet he had called home for 43 years (five of them spent in service to the Fuhrer's glorious Reich) was a mass of shattered rock pummeling the Moon.

As he pondered this disturbing scene, Deerhoven heard a voice.

"Wait until we tell the Fuhrer we have found the key to his victory over the Allied mongrels! For this, he will make us knights of the Iron Cross."

The voice was coming from nowhere and everywhere. For all he knew, it was inside his head. That is, if he had a head, which he didn't. He couldn't be sure, but he believed the mysterious voice belonged Dieter Roehm, his #1 assistant. Deerhoven sensed the presence of millions of people exactly like himself, free of bodily encumbrances, drifting among the fragments of their former planet.

He was no longer in his physical body; he was floating on the outside of a big, blue fish bowl looking in. How could he tell Hitler of this great triumph while in this condition?

As he looked around—though looking is hardly the word for someone without eyes—he witnessed an astonishing thing. Where planetary dust had circled the Moon moments ago, a perfectly formed Earth had miraculously taken its place, placidly adrift on a sea of stars. It looked exactly as it did before he pulled the lever destroying it. How could this be? Deerhoven wondered.

But, he had more pressing things to think about.

"*Was hast du getan, dummkopf?*" said another voice. This one he absolutely recognized. It was that of the Fuhrer himself, and it clanged like the chime of a church bell, a very angry church bell.

"Did I tell you to do this thing, you idiot? You and the others have been plotting against me! You have destroyed the Reich! Consider yourself under arrest. Germany will never capitulate! *Heil!*"

And yet, Deerhoven saw no Fuhrer. Even better, no Gestapo came to arrest him. His thoughts were: "What is Hitler doing here? What does this mean? Is Earth still here or is it not? Am I dead or am I alive?"

As he untangled his nettlesome thoughts, the Earth appeared to get larger. Either it was inflating to tremendous size, or Deerhoven was being pulled into it. He saw outlines of continents and rivers within the continents. Mountain ranges came into view. Roofs of houses appeared. He knew he was indeed returning to Earth!

That was when the hunger began. It was vague at first, since he had no body. And yet, hunger burned within. Trees came into view above a familiar hilltop. Below the trees, Deerhoven saw the enormous steel doors of his underground laboratory. The prodigal son had returned to Project Mind Fuhrer!

He passed through the tunnel's bombproof doors without the need to open them. Once inside, he followed a mile-long tunnel. The door to his laboratory, made of ten inch steel plate, was there too, as if nothing had changed. And, wonder of wonders, he was there, too.

Yes, Deerhoven, hard at work on Project Mind Fuhrer! How could this be? *He* was Deerhoven, not this interloper! His hunger grew stronger, a hunger for living flesh and a body to call his own. How he wanted to merge with this other Deerhoven—but how? There must be a way. When the human Deerhoven went to sleep that night, he would slip into the room and take his body away from him. He would live again.

That's when it struck him. Project Mind Fuhrer had transformed him into a DEADBEAT FROM ANOTHER DIMENSION!

17
Pulp Fiction Pariah

Drtikol's stories appeared in dime pulp magazines, the kind with lurid covers of half-naked babes being lowered into vats of hot wax by mad scientists. Thanks to my massive collection of science fiction magazines, I'd read most of Drtikol's hokey yarns.

His most famous character was Cornpone Freep, a door-to-door salesman from Kentucky. Freep appeared in nearly a dozen Drtikol stories. Off the top of my head, I remember a few.

In "Cornpone Freep and the Red Scare," (*Spicy Action Stories*, March 1945) Freep was canvassing the tiny river town of Paradise, Kentucky, peddling the Glo-in-the-Dark edition of the St. James Bible. We find Freep standing on a porch, making knuckle music on the door of the Paradise chapter of Young Republicans for Decency and Order. It was a dilapidated Antebellum house with a wrap-around front porch on a dead-end street. A heavy scent of mud from the Green River wafted through the humid air.

Freep had a well-rehearsed knock. It combined a friendly tap with the added authority of a city employee sent to warn of impending disaster. This unique rap brought customers to the door ninety percent of the time, and it worked this time, too.

A young woman answered the door. Except for a cross, painted upside down between her breasts, she was completely nude. Freep thought her lack of decorum unusual, even for a Republican, but members of the Grand Old Party, he mused, needed Glo-in-the-Dark Bibles as much as the Democrats, and so, he soldiered on.

"W-why, howdy, ma'am," Freep sputtered as he fought to keep his eyes on her pasty pan. "You look like a woman who does things a little different than other folks. I'd be willing to bet you're the kinda gal who'd go for this unique edition of..."

Before Freep could finish his pitch, which he'd practiced in front of his boarding house stand-up mirror, the naked woman grabbed him by the arm and exclaimed: "Why yes, young feller, of course I would!

My fellow Republicans and I are having a meeting about the upcoming primary elections. Why don't you come inside."

The woman wasn't exactly telling the truth. What Freep had stumbled onto was not a chapter of the Young Republicans for Decency and Order, but a coven of Satanists. Prior to Freep's fortuitous appearance, the group was lamenting their dwindling supply of townsfolk to sacrifice to Old Nick. That moved Freep to the front of the line.

Long story short, Freep escaped the Satanists and surrounded the house with Glo-in-the-dark Bibles. He then stretched out for a nap under a nearby pecan tree. No more than an hour later, the radium-infused Holy Word overpowered the Satanists. A broomstick with a white flag emerged from a broken windowpane. The devil worshippers surrendered to Freep's demands, which were: 1. Put on your clothes, 2. Renounce Satan, and 3. Stay away from Communists.

In "Don't Say No to Judy," (*Science Fiction Follies*, June 1945) Freep was tired of trudging door to door. Lucky for him, his next-door neighbor was the eccentric but affable Professor Gilmore Slipshod, who had helped Freep in previous adventures. Proudly thumb-tacked to Slipshod's front door was his mail-order diploma from the Biff-Klavis Inventor's University of Chicago, Illinois.

Freep pleaded for Slipshod's help. He needed time off to visit his sick uncle in El Segundo, California. After reading several *Popular Mechanics* articles on the future of robotics, Freep asked the kindly professor to construct a robot to take over his route. Slipshod agreed.

One week later, the Slipshod leaned out his window and squawked, "Cornpone! Come git your robot!"

Freep was overjoyed. He christened the robot, Judy McDangerboobs, so named for the Professor's lethal embellishment of rocket-fired warheads that doubled as the robot's bosom, seeing as how it was a female robot.

The problem, as always, was the Professor's absentmindedness. Slipshod forgot to program the meaning of the words NO THANK YOU into Judy McDangerboobs' robot brain. Thanks to Judy's bewilderment from refusals from front-porch customers, several bloody homicides followed.

How a mediocre pulp writer like Drtikol became the dreaded Ananda Vedanta was beyond me. Nevertheless, there were hints between the lines that a transformation was taking place, if you could keep reading this tripe long enough to dig them out.

The August 1945 issue of *Tortured Tales* featured Drtikol's, "The Man Who Brushed His Teeth Too Hard." The story barely hit newsstands when the Fresno chapter of the A. E. van Vogt Fan Club called for a boycott of both Drtikol and *Tortured Tales*. Fans found the story "disgusting," and buried the editor in a torrent of hate mail, demanding Drtikol be banished from *Tortured Tales* in perpetuity.

The protagonist in Drtikol's yarn was Adolf Hitler, who survived the war by fleeing to Pismo Beach, California, via U-boat. A plastic surgeon on board the sub gave Hitler a new face and a new name: Ambrose Itlerhay.

Being a fanatical vegetarian, Hitler, or rather, Itlerhay, opened Mein Tofu, a health food restaurant near the fishing pier on Pomeroy Street. Spoiler alert, the tofu contained an unexpected ingredient. Mayhem followed.

The editor of *Tortured Tales* blamed a disgruntled editorial assistant for accepting the story, and banned Franticek Drtikol stories forever. Drtikol believed a handful of science fiction fans were conspiring against him, and a growing paranoia began to infiltrate his work.

January 1947: *Stupendous Stories* published Drtikol's epic space opera, "Quo Valis," where the Nazis win WWII in an alternate universe by destroying Earth.

"Quo Valis" was a turning point in Drtikol's career. He claimed an extraterrestrial creature of infinite knowledge was beaming stories to him. Not only did Drtikol declare the stories were based on fact, he also proclaimed he knew more about the universe than Albert Einstein.

This was the last straw for the Fresno chapter of the A. E. van Vogt Fan Club. The plucky teenaged members organized a nationwide boycott of Biff-Klavis Publications, the parent company of *Stupendous Stories*.

Fans piled copies of Biff-Klavis magazines in town squares and burned them, while eager reporters covered the story. The club launched a massive letter-writing campaign directed at Harvey Biff, president of the Biff-Klavis publishing empire. The goal? Blackball Franticek Drtikol from Biff-Klavis.

In a heated letter to Harvey Biff, the president of the San Diego A. E. van Vogt Fan Club wrote: "*Not only does 'Quo Valis' refute Einstein's Theory of Relativity, it's just plain un-American!*"

The boycott gained steam and the call went out to all pulp magazine publishers: ban Franticek Drtikol ! As Carol Woodhouse of the Gary, Indiana Chapter of the A. E. van Vogt Fan Club wrote in her club newsletter *Forever Slans*:

We are fighting to make science fiction the crowning glory of the Atomic Age, not the laughingstock of serious literature! Franticek Drtikol writes dangerous nonsense that undermines the high standards of our beloved genre. Down with Drtikol! Up with true science fiction!

Biff-Klavis caved under the pressure. Drtikol became a pulp fiction pariah overnight. No magazine, no matter how sleazy, would touch him.

18
Hemet, California

The California Desert, August 1946:

The dark cloud that followed blacklisted writer Franticek Drtikol did have a silver lining. It stopped the flood of hate mail from angry science fiction fans. Once upon a time these vitriolic missives overflowed the Biff-Klavis mailroom. Now they barely made a trickle. The most recent letter, a straggler, was typical, and thankfully shorter than most:

Dear Mr. Drtikol, (if that's your real name)

I just finished reading 'Quo Valis' and have never read such balderdash in all my life. It's laughable that your "proof" for this "true" story is your claim that it came to you through a supernatural source. I suspect your "source" was a medical condition brought on from smoking too much devil weed.

Eat death, Nazi Scum,
Norm Kossuth, Barstow Chapter, A. E. van Vogt Fan Club

Besides fan mail, Drtikol faced other serious threats. High on the list was his inability to pay the rent at the Indian Rock Bungalow Court, where he lived in the small desert town of Hemet.

A 30-day eviction notice appeared on his front door while he was shopping at the Indian Rock Food 'n Booze. The notice fluttered menacingly in the asthmatic desert wind.

"This wasn't here when I left, dammit," Drtikol snapped. He tore off the notice and kicked open the door with his size 15 shoe.

"Maybe I'll have to give up writing and find a real job," he thought. But doing what? He knew nothing of work, as the lower classes understood it. He was born for better things.

He placed a solitary tin of Heinz 57 baked beans on his kitchen table. This was breakfast, lunch, and dinner, unless he found something else to hock. He laid the hungry swivel on his Remington typewriter.

"Looks like you're next, old girl," Drtikol wheezed, his lungs clogged with desert sand. He'd already pawned everything of value at the Indian Rock Loan Company; everything but the Remington.

Just as his writing career hit rock bottom, Fate stepped in. Franticek Drtikol did not know it then, but he was about to join an exclusive club whose members are religious prophets. He would ascend to another world, from down-and-out science fiction writer to barefoot seer, with thousands of devoted followers—and money; lots and lots of money.

As with most spiritual transformations, Drtikol's came from beyond human comprehension. In his case, it was a meddling alien from another planet.

How this creature came to be in Hemet was a long story, but it didn't take long before it moved into Drtikol's bungalow to escape the desert sun. Once inside, it set up camp in a corner of the kitchen ceiling, where it had a clear view of his typing desk. Drtikol didn't notice his tiny, freeloading roommate, but even if he had, he would have seen nothing more than a common spider.

19
Unktomia

The spider wasn't just frittering away its time on Drtikol's kitchen ceiling. It was studying its new roommate. The lanky pulp writer was just one of many Earth creatures that lived nearby, and the spider was interested in all of them. It spun a telaug to keep track.

A telaug resembled a typical spider's web, but on Unktomia, the spider's home planet, a telaug can telepathically augment (tel-aug, get it?) the spider's nerve center; sort of like a giant antenna with extra features.

Using its telaug, the spider could project its etheric body anywhere in the world while simultaneously lounging on the kitchen ceiling in Hemet. The telaug also had a remote viewing feature called a penetray, a useful tool that allowed the spider to study the index card catalog at the public library in downtown Hemet. It had a universal language translator, too. The spider activated that right off.

The first book it read using penetray was *How to Win Friends and Influence People* by Napoleon Hill. Thus, the spider learned how to understand Earth creature behavior. It had no interest in taking over the planet. All it wanted was to be somewhere else, having landed in California by accident, after a strange series of events.

Its starship, resembling a dandelion's fluffy, white seed sail, fell to Earth when its atomic fuel cell hit Empty. Unktomian fuel cells have a half-life of 500,000 years, and the spider's ship conked out at the very moment a small, watery planet called Earth appeared on its view screen. A few hasty flight corrections, and the spider set course for a controlled crash landing.

That was when all hell broke loose. In a flash, the blue planet exploded. As the spider watched in horror, its landing site turned into a clump of glowing embers.

"Dammit!" the spider cursed, though this was a loose translation. "I'm running on fumes! Now what?"

The spider hurriedly calculated its odds for survival. They were zero. As if the spider couldn't be more surprised, it was. The planet suddenly reappeared, turning slowly on its axis, as if nothing had happened. The spider rubbed all 26 of its eyes, but still could not believe it.

"What just happened? I know I've been in space for 500,001 years; maybe I've finally come down with space madness."

The spider's landing coordinates were still locked onto its original landing site, so the ship continued its descent, touching down in the California desert.

The spider had witnessed a once-in-a-thousand-lifetimes event: an Inter-dimensional Planet Swap.

One major side effect of the Planet Swap was a case of mass amnesia among the planet's inhabitants. This was likely a coping mechanism to help the primitive human brain adjust. It meant that no one other than the spider knew what had just happened, which put the spider in a unique position. It had valuable information.

Stranded, and out of touch with its home planet, the spider's primary concern was fuel and how to get more of it. Seated at the ship's instrument panel, the tiny arachnid began waving its appendages over colorful translucent buttons resembling the heads of insects. There were buttons in the shape of wasps, beetles, earwigs, and some that had no relation to bugs on Earth.

Its instruments indicated the inhabitants below had a crude knowledge of atomic fission, which meant they must have access to plutonium. The most expeditious way to get this fuel, the spider thought, was convince the creatures to offer it willingly. This would require further planning.

20
The Spider and the Fly by Night

Franticek Drtikol's downward spiral continued at a heady pace. Food seemed like a comforting idea, so he picked up the can of Heinz 57 baked beans to prepare supper. As he jabbed the can opener into the lid, a far-off squeal caught his attention.

"Must be my tinnitus acting up again," he muttered to himself. But when he began to make out words that sounded like English, he listened closer.

"Hey, Shakespeare! Up here," the voice squeaked like a mouse on helium. Drtikol's head tweaked one way, then the other. He studied the light fixture on the ceiling, saw nothing unusual, and went back to his supper. The voice persisted.

"Are you deaf?" it screeched. "I'm up here, in the corner, over the sink!"

Drtikol looked again, frowning. He squinted at the sink.

"Dirty dishes," he grumbled. "I'll leave those for my stupid landlord."

His gaze moved from the sink to the wall to the ceiling. A spider web clinging to the cupboard caught his attention. A spider reclined in the center of the web.

He'd never noticed this spider before; then again, why would he? Maybe he should take a broom and get rid of it.

"Bah, who cares? I'm leaving this dump anyway," he said, staring at the spider. But the bug on the ceiling stared back. He felt strangely uneasy.

Come to think of it, he'd never seen a spider quite like it. It had an orange body the size of dried prune. It had green eyes and purplish legs. He studied the spider carefully, starting with the legs. He counted ten.

"That's funny," he thought. "Spiders have eight legs."

The spider, responding to Drtikol's thought, replied: "On my planet, we have ten, not eight. For a writer, you're not very observant. Isn't that what writers are supposed to do, observe? You've completely ignored me for one entire orbit around your planet's power source. Not too observant, I'd say."

Drtikol froze like a zipper on a cheap pair of pants. Did the spider just speak to him? Maybe his readers were right. Maybe he was mad, and the spider was part of his madness. It didn't exist. How could it?

"Oh, but I do," the contrary spider replied, having read Drtikol's thoughts a second time. "But don't worry. I won't tell anyone you've spoken to me, if that's what bothers you."

Feeling like a fool for talking to a spider, Drtikol replied: "H-how do I know y-you exist outside my imagination?"

"Because you have no imagination," the spider replied. "I've read your stories. You never would have thought me up in a million years. But never mind that. Not only can I prove I exist, I'll be your mentor, your benefactor. You do need help, don't you?"

"What can you do for me? You're a spider."

"Has a spider ever spoken to you before?"

"Well, no."

"I rest my case! And I can do a lot more than speak, ugly Earth thing. I can make you famous. Answer me this: do you enjoy being a washed-up writer?"

"I must be out of my mind," Drtikol mumbled. "Say, what do you mean, washed up? I've written some fantastic stories."

The spider wheezed a tiny cough laugh. "No one else seems to think so. Your career didn't take off until I wrote 'Quo Valis.'"

"Baloney!" Drtikol spat. "I typed that story in this very room, on that typewriter!" He pointed a bony finger at his Remington.

"Yes, you did a great job, too; hardly any typos," the spider replied. "But I put the words into your brain. I based that story on true events, something I witnessed as I approached your downtrodden planet. Naturally you don't remember it, but your entire planet and everyone on it blew up, just like in the story."

Drtikol remained skeptical. "If this planet and everyone on it were destroyed, that would include me. But here I am, talking to you. You're crazy!"

"Don't be so negative," the spider said. "Your imagination is still limping along in first gear. 'Quo Valis' was heading to the top of the charts until those so-called fans of yours started making noise about you being a nut ball."

"Yeah, and a Communist and a cannibal," Drtikol added. "So, don't do me any more favors, okay? I couldn't get a job writing fortunes for a Chinese cookie factory, thanks to you."

"You're whining, Drtikol, snap out of it!"

"This can't be happening," Drtikol groaned, covering his face with his hands. "That can of beans gave me ptomaine poisoning. That's it! You're the result of a spoiled can of baked beans."

"Still not convinced, eh?" the spider squeaked. "Let's try a different approach. What if I tell you exactly what will happen to you if you step outside your front door. Would that convince you?"

"It might, unless this is just my stressed out unconscious mind."

"Give me a break, Hemmingway! Now listen. As soon as you step outside that door, the little Earthling larva in bungalow number two will come up to you and say: 'Have you seen my dog, Mr. Drtikol?' Is that simple enough?"

"Dunno. I suppose."

Drtikol had been obsessing over the fragility of his mental state for weeks. This might well be the psychotic break he feared was coming. Then again, what did he have to lose, other than his mind, which may be lost already? He shuffled outside into the desert sun and saw no one. He walked to the carport where he used to park his 1927 Hupmobile. The carport was empty. He'd sold the car for $25 to pay last month's bills.

He was about to walk back to his studio apartment when a child's voice said: "Have you seen my dog, Mr. Drtikol?" The writer spun around to see Timmy, the boy from bungalow number two. Drtikol was so flummoxed, his voice cracked.

"S-sorry, T-T-immy I, NO, I haven't seen him," he stammered, and rushed at full gallop to his bungalow to confirm the spider's prediction.

He returned to the spot where the spider had harangued him moments ago. No spider. Even the cobweb was gone.

"That does it," Drtikol thought to himself. "Next stop, Camarillo State Hospital. The wheels have come off and I'll never get them back on again."

"Don't you ever get tired of listening to yourself?" a familiar squeak said. The spider had relocated. It was hanging above the typewriter. "What do you say now? Still skeptical?"

Begrudgingly, Drtikol replied: "I guess I'll have to believe you, after what just happened. How did you...?"

"Never mind that!" The spider barked. "We have to restart your career, and with your reputation that won't be easy. First, I want you to go to the stationery store and bring back a fresh typewriter ribbon. I know, I know, you're broke. Look in the coin return bucket of the public phone outside the office, you'll find 25¢. You've got some serious typing to do. Now, get going!"

Drtikol ran to the phone, and just like the spider said, he found a quarter in the return bucket. He took the quarter to Indian Rock Stationery and bought a fresh typewriter ribbon for the Remington. Back in his bungalow, he threaded this new ribbon into the typewriter and waited for his muse. The spider wasted no time.

Possessed by the alien arachnid's superior mind, Dritkol's fingers flew across the keys in a white-hot blur. Drtikol tried to catch a few winks of sleep now and then, but the spider lived in a state of perpetual twilight, and didn't need to sleep.

Drtikol typed and typed and when he was finished he had the sequel to "Quo Valis." The spider called the finished manuscript, "Why Skeets Malloy Has Two Heads." It was typical space opera, full of half-baked Earth pre-history and occult mysticisms. It picked up the saga of Project Mind Fuhrer where "Quo Valis" left off, revealing the story of a planet populated by amnesiacs.

The North American boycott of Drtikol's work compelled the blacklisted writer to find sympathetic editors in foreign countries. He found one in Argentina. The story appeared as "¿Por qué Skeets Malloy Tiene Dos Cabezas?" in the December 1946 issue of *Cuentos Sangrientos (Bloody Tales)* a lurid Buenos Aires pulp magazine with right wing sympathies.

Drtikol's spirits soared. And because *Cuentos Sangrientos* paid its writers on acceptance, he was able to pay his landlord the back rent and a month in advance. Drtikol's icebox overflowed with frozen dinners. Life was good again.

The spider's prediction had come true. Drtikol was a successful pulp writer again; at least in South America.

21
The Plan

Franticek Drtikol was gorging himself on a re-warmed turkey and mashed potatoes One-Eyed Eskimo frozen dinner when the spider interrupted his reverie. It was time to begin the next phase of the spider's plan. Transferring thoughts into Drtikol's mind, the spider said:

"Stop stuffing your nutrient orifice and start thinking about your future!"

Drtikol looked surprised.

"Future?" he mumbled, barely audible through a mouthful of apple crisp. "We're doing great! I'm going straight to the top! I'll be a keynote speaker at the science fiction convention this year, no doubt about it."

The spider would have looked disgusted if it had a face.

"Are you telling me you'd forgive those ungrateful science fiction fans after what they did to you?" the spider squeaked. "They made your life a living hell! Forget their stupid convention! You need to take this to the next level. Why not found your own religion? Convince the other humans that you hold all the secrets! You could be a great and powerful leader."

"I don't see where this is going," Drtikol gurgled as he swilled another can of beer.

"Think about it," the spider wheedled. "Only you and I know your stories are based on fact, and the fact is, Earth was destroyed and somehow reborn. The only reason you know that is because I saw it happen and told you about it. No one else knows Deadbeats from old Earth are still out there, sucking souls on new Earth. This is the stuff holy books are made of! You'll be the first prophet of the Atomic Age. Show your readers how to save themselves! You've got all the answers!"

Drtikol drifted in and out of a mild trance. He was under the spider's spell, mulling over the religion angle when the spider spiked the ball.

"We'll call it Omenon, the Phen-Omenon of the New Age!" the spider cheered. "And you'll begin by writing the third installment of the

"Quo Valis" trilogy. It will be the instruction manual for the Omenon movement."

As it wandered through Drtikol's mind checking the engine, kicking the tires, the spider discovered the writer's self-absorbed, authoritarian tendencies. Its proposal would be hard for the Earthling to resist, and it knew it.

Suddenly, Drtikol made up his mind. He would do it! He tossed his empty TV dinner tray into the trash and galloped outside to his 1940 Oldsmobile, purchased with the proceeds from his latest pulp sales. He thumbed the starter and took off at high speed to Indian Rock Stationery, where he purchased a ream of typing paper and two new typewriter ribbons.

Returning to his bungalow, he threaded the freshly inked ribbon into the Remington and began typing. His writing method was simple: let his mind go blank and let the spider do the thinking.

The result was, "I Remember Earth!" Unborn generations would study and squabble over the story for decades, if not centuries to come. Drtikol stood in front of a cracked mirror in his bedroom and imagined his new "look." Classic paintings of iconic religious figures came to mind. The default look seemed to be a billowing robe, long hair and beard, and bare feet.

"If it was good enough for Moses," Drtikol said to his reflection in the mirror, "it's good enough for me."

Next day, he drove to the San Jacinto Rexall drugstore and slid inside a phone booth. He thumbed through the Yellow Pages until he found Costume Supplies. He tore out a full page ad for Reginald's Costume Warehouse in North Hollywood. The ad said Reginald specialized in Biblical epics of the Cecil B. DeMille variety. Drtikol wasted no time. He hopped back into the Olds and souped the cylinders; destination: North Hollywood.

Reginald found the perfect robe for Drtikol's look, the only "extra tall" robe he had in stock, seeing as how the fledgling guru was seven feet tall. The rest of the outfit was easy; long hair and a beard he could grow for free.

In the not-too-distant future, Drtikol would order custom made robes, woven by Tibetan monks in a remote Himalayan monastery. He found the monks through an article in *Amazing Stories* titled, "The Mystery Monks of Tibet" by Vincent Gaddis.

The spider, however, was about to learn the hard way what a bad idea this would turn out to be.

22
Deadbeats and Comebacks

After reading my copy of "Quo Valis," I went back to my pulp collection for the next installment in the trilogy: "¿Por Qué Skeets Malloy Tiene Dos Cabezas?"

The title sounded innocent enough, only because I couldn't read Spanish. Paloma was fluent in Spanish as well as Chinese, so she translated while the Prof and I smoked and listened.

"Do you want it word for word," Paloma asked, "or the *Reader's Digest* version?"

"Skip the hyperbole and just dole out the highlights," I replied. "I can only take so much Drtikol."

Paloma obliged, using Spanish words only when English wouldn't suffice.

"So, this Skeets Malloy was a two-headed sideshow performer in a traveling circus," she began. "The reason Deadbeats didn't suck Malloy's soul was because of the complicated retinal circuitry that made up his two heads. It was too confusing for the Deadbeats to figure out.

"Skeets wasn't his, or their, real name. They had two other names. The right head was called Hindenburg, and the left was Zeppelin. They got top billing in the Yerxa Brothers Circus sideshow. The finale of their act was a performance of the Papageno/Papagena duet from Mozart's "The Magic Flute." Hindenburg sang soprano, Zeppelin sang baritone. This always brought down the house.

"But the sideshow was just a part-time gig, see, a way to support themselves at MIT, where they studied nuclear physics. Regardless of what others thought, having two heads was a plus for Skeets, who graduated in half the time of the average one-headed student. After graduation they ditched their sideshow gig for a job with the US atomic weapons program."

"When Deadbeats made Comebacks out of everyone, Skeets got lonely, being surrounded by so many Deadbeat-controlled Comebacks."

"Hold it right there, Kitten," I yawned. "What the hell is a Comeback?"

"A Comeback is a human that's been taken over by a Deadbeat. Skeets was the only non-Comeback human left. Anyway, Skeets came up with a plan to rid the world of Deadbeats and put everything right again."

"Good grief," I grouched.

The Professor stopped puffing his pipe long enough to explain.

"It may sound crazy to us," he said, "but Ananda Vedanta's followers believe every word of it. Sure, it's a story in a dime pulp magazine, but they believe it holds hidden truths. In any case, please continue, Miss Liu."

"While rummaging through the stacks at the Detroit Public Library," Paloma went on, "Hindenburg and Zeppelin find an ancient scroll about Lemuria, an ancient lost continent that sunk off the California coast, sort of like Atlantis."

Dvorak interrupted her.

"This part of the plot segues into the third part of Drtikol's trilogy, "Yo Recuerdo Terra." (I Remember Earth)" the Professor said. "The scroll described the ancient Lemurians, who used incredibly advanced technology to rule the world."

I groaned. "So, this is the baloney Ananda Vedanta teaches his suckers?"

"One must never underestimate the human mind," he lectured. "The urge to believe in the unbelievable is difficult to resist. Please continue, Miss Liu."

"Okay, blah, blah, blah, Hindenburg and Zeppelin locate the real Lemuria, and surround it with atomic bombs of their own design. Don't forget, they're nuclear physicists. Zeppelin pushes the button that detonates the bombs in sequence. Slowly, the sea parts and Lemuria rises, revealing the once glorious capital city of Hel.

"After recovering an array of Lemurian technology, Skeets uses a mind ray on the Deadbeat interlopers, freeing enslaved human minds and banishing the Deadbeats to distant space. A joyous populace crowns Skeets Malloy King of the World. Lemuria becomes the center of power of New Earth. The End."

I snubbed out my Chesterfield in the ash stand.

"So, this is why Vedanta's been collecting nuclear material," I said. "To raise Lemuria. I knew it had to be in there somewhere."

"Or what he thinks is Lemuria," the Professor replied. "He didn't build that bunker in Pt. Reyes on a whim. He chose that spot for a reason."

I said, "If he's planning atomic Armageddon, the Feds should know about this, Professor. You've got to go public."

Dvorak shook his head.

"I'm afraid it would be my word against Vedanta's," he countered, "as well as a few hundred Freeps and Galactic Rangers that would back him up. Besides, once I come out of hiding, I'm a dead man. Come to think of it, now that you have this information, your lives are in danger as well."

"There's one big difference, Professor," I said. "As far as Vedanta's concerned, you're dead. Being deceased means you can't tell us anything."

"In that case," the Prof replied, "find that radioactive material before it's too late. From what I overheard last month, Vedanta's bombs weren't operational, but close. The smoking gun is the plutonium. When you find out where they're keeping it, we've got proof."

"I'll check out the Lemurian angle, too," I said. "Like you say, there has to be a reason Vedanta bought that property."

"You're in luck," Dvorak said, using his Kaywoodie as an exclamation point. "The leading authority on the Pt. Reyes area is Dr. Eric Pangloss, of Bolinas. That's only twenty minutes from Pt. Reyes Station. Pangloss and I became friends before the war, when we met at a seminar in Big Sur. I'm sure he's heard about my death by now. He also knows my daughter. She can introduce you to Pangloss."

23
How to Make a Freep

Ananda Vedanta was in a foul mood. He was guiding a group of neophytes through an emotional minefield called The Purge. This Purge took place on a ridge overlooking the northern California coast. The view was impressive. Barely visible to the south was San Francisco and its Golden Gate. To the north, Tomales Point.

The glorious panorama did nothing to temper the self-proclaimed guru's negative vibrations. He was having a temper tantrum he liked to call his "Ex-Lax Energizer," so named for the emotional dump his

Ananda Vedanta

neophytes had to take before enlightenment came knocking on their thick skulls.

"No, No, No, you worthless piles of cow dung!" Vedanta screeched, coughing up a tonsil. "You are weaklings! Less than scum! You cannot attain Free Consciousness until you divest yourselves of the Deadbeats within. Don't you GET THAT?!"

Deadbeats were bad news. When a Deadbeat locked on to your soul, you were subservient to the Old Ways. Even without a Deadbeat, the life of a neophyte was no bed of roses. Members called these mandatory Purge sessions "the chicken yard," so named because they pecked relentlessly at each other's inner Deadbeat until petty egos crumbled. Once free of the Deadbeat, a neophyte became a full-fledged, unquestioning Freep, named after Drtikol's goofy pulp hero Cornpone Freep.

In today's Purge, a young neophyte cowered at the bare feet of his guru master. The neophyte's shaved head symbolized subservience to Omenon, and everyone knew that Ananda Vedanta *was* Omenon. Conforming to a strict dress code, a neophyte wore bib overalls over red, woolen long johns. These were uncomfortable, but that was the point. It made the neophytes keenly aware of their inner Deadbeat.

A short distance away, two German gunsels leaned against Vedanta's brand new Kaiser Deluxe Jade Dragon parked on Mt. Vision Rd. They bantered in Kraut, smoked Kraut cigarettes, and never took their Aryan optics off the narrow road in front of them. A few short years ago, they were card-carrying Nazis in Heinrich Himmler's infamous SS. Now they enjoyed the California climate as members of Omenon's elite Galactic Rangers.

Their job was to protect the self-styled guru whenever he left his bunker to dwell among the Norms, those unenlightened citizens who had not yet become Freeps.

Few cars drove this remote one lane road over Mt. Vision. It connected Old Lighthouse Road on the coast with Sir Francis Drake highway inland.

Sir Francis was a well-known name in Pt. Reyes. So much so that he had a beach and a highway named after him. He had dropped anchor off the Pt. Reyes peninsula in 1579, proclaiming California for Queen Elizabeth I. He called it New Albion. That meant nothing to the Miwoks who already lived here. It also meant nothing to the German gunsels standing on Mt. Vision Road.

Locals knew of the secretive cult on the mountain and stayed away. Those who got too close were pulled aside by Galactic Rangers and dished out enough grief to put them in traction for a month.

Wrapping up his Purge, Vedanta growled, "You're nothing but a bunch of Comeback losers! You've got some serious DDT* to accomplish today." (*DDT–Deadbeat Decoupling Treatment). "No more games, or I'll throw you in the sheep dip at the next Purge. Dismissed!"

Vedanta's lofty seven-foot frame added weight to his threats. His gray woolen robe billowed as he walked. He moved as if celestial forces guided him. His long, black hair and beard were in stark contrast to the clean-cut local ranchers, whose fashion sense leaned toward flannel shirts, jeans, and rubber galoshes.

With long, determined strides, Vedanta approached his Kaiser Dragon as his bodyguard opened the rear door. He climbed in, careful not to hit his head. The Kaiser barely had enough headroom to contain his lanky frame.

"To the bunker," he wheezed, visibly exhausted from The Purge.

"Yah, Mind Fuhrer," the driver yeeped. He made a three-point turn on the narrow road, heading back down Mt. Vision Road to Omenon headquarters. Ananda Vedanta leaned back into the plush, mohair upholstery and lit a Lucky Strike, his favorite brand, inhaling until his lungs reached their limit.

His neophytes, on the other hand, began their pathetic return to the compound on bare feet. They were lucky the Holy One didn't make them crawl on their hands and knees. He'd done that before.

Vedanta was a rare sight in the small town of Pt. Reyes Station. He had no need for it. A narrow-gauge railroad made regular stops there twenty years ago, but automobile travel put an end to that. He had an army of Freeps to do his bidding, and Galactic Rangers to enforce Omenon law. His reinforced concrete bunker could withstand an atomic blast or a lengthy standoff with local law enforcement. He'd stockpiled enough food and ammunition to last a year.

24
No Progress on the Astral Plane

The Chief was snoring loudly under my Navy surplus desk when I entered the office. The snoring annoyed me, but not half as much as what he had done to the office. He had removed the TV chassis from its Bakelite cabinet and surrounded it with tiny conch shells on the floor. He had replaced the vacuum tubes with tail feathers from a large brown bird, and the tubes were now standing upright in a circle in the waiting room. A crow's skull sat in the center of the circle. My jaw, and the wheezer in my kisser, hit the floor.

"What the hell in blue blazes happened to my new television set?" I roared.

The Chief's head popped up from under the desk like a prairie dog from its den.

"Oh, great white hunter return," the Chief said in his nasal monotone. "Chief in middle of twenty-four hour incantation. Making good progress. Fu Manchu in teevee having tough time climbing over Chief's obstacle course."

"I don't have the energy for this conversation," I groaned. "Just stick with it,

Chief. And make sure you put that television set back the way you found it. Paloma gets real testy if she misses Big Time Wrestling, especially this week. It's a Christmas grudge match: Gorgeous George vs. Santa's Slay."

I left post haste to avoid blowing another head gasket, but not before I touched bases with the Dvorak damsel. She had to arrange a meeting with Pangloss, the geologist.

I used Paloma's phone to dial the Dvorak mansion. The maid, Mai Ling, picked up. I told her who was calling. She put down the receiver and got lost to locate the Dvorak quail. Before I could lay a torch to another Chesterfield Isabelle was on the blower.

"Why, Alex," she gushed. "What a pleasant surprise."

"Keep your sweater on, Princess, and I mean it. This is strictly a business call. I'm about to make some headway on your father's case.

Can you set up a meeting with a geologist named Dr. Pangloss? He's one of your dad's old pals. I need answers to some geological type questions."

"Is that all you think about, Alex—geology? In that case, I know a mine you could explore."

"Your kind of geology has nothing to do with rocks, Isabelle."

"If you put your mind to it, it might. Okay, I'll bite! What does Dr. Pangloss, a geologist, have to do with Father's case?"

"That's something we'll both find out from Pangloss. Can you arrange it?"

"Of course. When do we go?"

"As soon as you set it up. Now, here's the plan. I'll wait for you in San Anselmo at the seminary. I don't want that blue Chrysler that's parked outside your house to follow us. I'll park my heap behind Montgomery Hall, facing away from the parking lot. Do you know where that is?"

"Yes, father lectured there a few times."

"Good. Park your car in front of Montgomery Hall. Enter through the front doors and exit through the back door. I'll be waiting for you behind the building. If the Chrysler shows up, they'll keep watch on your car. But you won't be coming back out, see? It's the old bait and switch."

"What fun! It's just like the movies," Isabelle thrilled.

"And do me a favor," I said.

"Yes, of course."

"Wear a skirt that falls below your knees."

25
Bolinas

I chain smoked and waited behind Montgomery Hall for the Dvorak nympho to arrive. From here I could see any car entering the parking lot. If Omenon was tailing her, I'd know.

Montgomery Hall was a high-class rock pile built in the last century. It had castle-like towers and fancy stone carvings above windows tall enough to stack eight tiny reindeer one on top of another. Students had returned home for Christmas, so the campus was empty.

Then, headlamp beams raked the overhanging oak trees near the road. Isabelle's yellow bull-nosed Packard rolled onto the Seminary parking lot in a whisper of all eight cylinders. She was heading to Montgomery Hall, as I instructed. Ten seconds later, a dark blue Chrysler sedan followed. The Dvorak quail stuck to the plan. She parked her car, entered through the front of the building, exited through the back door, and climbed inside my waiting heap.

Also as requested, she had cocooned her curves inside a green, ankle-length wool dress she must have painted on. A belt tightened a waist-length light brown leather coat. Her round fur hat made her look like a blonde Cossack.

"I do hope this conforms to your Puritanical dress code," she purred as she slid her caboose in my direction. I looked her over.

"Perfect," I said. "Now, lay down on the seat. We've got to leave without them seeing you."

"You mean I've been followed?" she quavered, and bent down, resting her head on my lap. I was tingling in places I didn't want to think about.

"Not exactly what I had in mind," I cringed, "but it'll have to do."

We cruised through the parking lot in low gear, exiting onto the one lane road that snaked down Seminary Hill. I checked the rear-vision mirror. The blue car stayed put.

"No wonder they lost the war," I snorted. "Okay, Miss Dvorak, you can sit up now."

"Do I have to? And would you please stop the Miss Dvorak jazz! I thought we'd reached a degree of, well, intimacy. After all, you did manhandle my boobs."

"I realize that," I replied in a businesslike tone. "But this isn't a movie, as much as you'd like to think it is. We need to stay focused."

"What if you can't resist me and it happens all over again?"

"It won't happen again, Isabelle. Indiscretions are a distraction we can't afford. This case is dangerous to everyone involved, including you."

"That's what I don't understand," she said, lifting her head off my thigh. "What exactly is this danger? I mean, I guess I'm being followed, but why?"

"Your father felt that someone, most likely Ananda Vedanta, was trying to kill him, which is why he wrote that letter to Fu Chan. Maybe Vedanta is keeping an eye on you to make sure you father is really dead. Remember, this guy is one mean messiah. He even keeps a harem of female devotees to soothe his deepest spiritual yearnings, if you get my drift."

"It sounds like a movie, Alex. I'm sure I saw one just like that."

"It's not a movie! I'm a detective," I growled. "I know."

The conversation dragged on like this as we cruised down the defunct railroad line that had turned into the Sir Francis Drake highway. We passed through Yolanda Station, Landsdale Station, and finally, Fairfax, the final stop before Pt. Reyes Station.

West Marin is rolling hills and wide-open ranch land. From boredom, the cattle eat low hanging leaves off the solitary oak trees, giving them a neatly trimmed look. Sir Francis Drake dead-ends at the Petaluma–Pt. Reyes Road, where we turned left and headed toward the coast.

The air began to smell like the sea, and dense forests of oak and bay laurel trees hid the hills. Somehow the road turned into Sir Francis Drake again, and we followed it into the tiny town of Olema. From there, the coast highway snaked through Dogtown and a series of stomach-churning downhill curves. The thirteenth turn dropped us at Horseshoe Hill Road that took us straight into Bolinas.

We passed a cemetery with a church, a general store, and the town's one gasoline pump. Modest Victorian homes lined Wharf Road, the town's main street. As we passed The Schooner Saloon, the Dvorak canary began to warble.

"Oh, please, please! I need a drink!" she bleated. "Let's try that saloon over there for a quickie."

I made a sharp U-turn. The Hudson's wide wheelbase nearly knocked down a picket fence on the other side of the road. We parked in front of the saloon and we got out and stretched.

"These country roads aren't meant for the squeamish," I complained, rubbing the small of my back. "Or for cars like a Hudson Commodore."

Bolinas looked like a Hollywood Western movie set. The Schooner Saloon, built during the Gold Rush, was a whitewashed clapboard box with a small, overhung front porch above two swing doors. The sidewalk was made of worn wooden boards. Inside, three fishermen in faded pea coats were playing gin rummy at a table near the door. The rosewood bar looked like it had sailed around the horn 100 years ago.

A bartender with a long, gray hair and handlebar mustache stopped polishing shot glasses long enough to greet us. His apron was too short. Maybe it belonged to his grandkid.

"Come on in, folks," the codger welcomed. "Where you hail from? Ross? San Anselmo?"

"Ross," I said. "What gave us away?"

"The young lady's mink hat. Not a common sight in these parts. Oh, and that bulge under your left arm says you're not here for the sea air."

"You're very observant," I said. "I'd be willing to bet you can tell us what drinks we want, too."

"I'll take that bet," the bartender snickered.

Clearing his throat, he laid the beady eye on Isabelle for five seconds.

"Gin martini with a splash of vermouth for the lady. And for the gunsel, let me see. Jack Daniels on the rocks with a beer chaser. How'd I do?"

Isabelle looked shocked, as if the barkeep had used X-Ray Specs to view her panties.

"Jeez Louise, this guy is good!" she gawked. "I'll take that gin martini please, with a pimiento-stuffed green olive."

"And you, sir?"

"Vat 69, one ice cube, with a splash of tonic."

"Oh, a contrarian," the bartender replied.

He turned to a shelf behind the bar to fetch bottles of Vat 69 and Beefeaters. He excused himself to search for a jar of stuffed green olives in the back room. After placing our drinks on paper napkins, he began to chat, like bartenders often do in small towns. Maybe it's idle curiosity, and maybe it's just plain nosiness.

"What brings you to the boondocks?" he pumped, swiping the bar with a towel to look casual.

"One of your illustrious citizens," I replied. "Dr. Eric Pangloss. We've got an appointment with him. How do we find Brighton Avenue?"

"Dr. Pangloss, eh? I'd heard he was back in town for the holidays. Well, it's pretty hard to get lost in Bolinas, young feller. When you get back to your car, drive back out the same way you come in. When you see a white church on the corner, take a left. That's Brighton. It'll take you all the way to Brighton Beach if you keep on going. But you'll only need to drive a few blocks. The Pangloss house is the first on your right after you pass the tennis court."

"There's a tennis court here?" I yelped. The codger got a hurt look on his mush.

"Tennis ain't just for the idle rich, you know. Some of us hicks can even play chess. A few of us own televisions, too."

"No offense, brother," I said. "I was just surprised a town this size had a tennis court."

Isabelle Dvorak downed her martini while the bartender yakked. Holding out her empty glass at arm's length, she asked the barkeep: "How 'bout filling my stocking, Santa?"

The bartender laid the heavy swivel on her.

"I'd say you done a pretty good job of that all by yourself, young lady," he snickered.

As he reached for her glass, I barked: "Belay that second martini, bartender! We're running late."

"You're no fun." She pouted, pulling on her gloves.

I paid the bartender and gave him a generous tip.

"Come back anytime," he grinned. "Folks from Ross are always welcome in Bolinas. And bring your tennis racket next time!"

I'd parked the Hudson aimed in the right direction. We'd barely started moving when I lamped the corner church. As instructed, we turned left and, just like the codger said, Brighton curved gently toward the beach. We parked next to the tennis court.

The Pangloss home was at the far end of a long, narrow front yard surrounded by hedges. The house looked like a Swiss chalet, contrasting with the modest Victorian homes that lined Brighton Avenue. I closed the weathered gate behind us and we followed the brick path to a green front door. A festive holly wreath ringed a leaded glass peephole in the door. I knocked. We didn't wait long before Pangloss answered.

Pangloss was about 60. He had a graying goatee, wire-rimmed specs, and wore two Argyle sweaters, one on top of the other. The outside sweater was red, the inner one was green. Written in black ink on the tops of his leather moccasins were the words RIGHT and LEFT. No wonder they call these eggheads absent-minded.

"Ah, Mr. Blade," the jolly geologist quacked as he stood on the doorsill. "And Isabelle! It's been so long! You were in pigtails the last time I saw you. I was heartbroken to hear about your father. It was all so dreadful. I shall miss him."

"Thank you," Isabelle replied, adding, "Yes, it's been a long time."

Pangloss ushered us into the living room, where a blazing fire crackled in a rustic stone fireplace made of black chunks of obsidian amid smooth river rock. We sat in overstuffed chairs, warming ourselves in front of the fire. Coastal Marin is cold and damp this time of year, so the fire was a welcome sight.

"I must admit, Isabelle, your call intrigued me," the Professor began. Then he turned to me. "But why would Mr. Blade be so anxious to see me?"

"I'm not sure of that myself," Isabelle said, "but I think we're about to find out. Alex, I mean Mr. Blade, is a private detective working on behalf of Father's manservant, Fu Chan. Fu Chan reopened father's case. There were unusual circumstances about the accident, I'm told."

Pangloss looked surprised. "Reopened? Why would Fu Chan want to reexamine your father's accident?"

"Dr. Dvorak spelled out my involvement in a sealed letter he left for Fu Chan," I explained. "It was to be opened only in the event the Professor's death was suspicious. Fu Chan believed it was. Long story short, the Professor wanted his killer brought to justice. That's where I come in."

The geologist's jaw dropped like a sack of rocks. "I think this is where I'm supposed to ask, 'What does this have to do with me?'"

"Your knowledge of the Pt. Reyes area could help me with a potential angle," I said. "Is there anything unusual about this place, geologically speaking?"

"Geologically speaking, it's marvelous," the Professor replied. "Not only does the San Andreas Fault pass directly under Tomales Bay, but the geological footprint of Pt. Reyes differs significantly from the rest of California."

"How so?" I asked.

"Before the war, a group of Japanese geologists came here to study our peninsula. They found an uncanny resemblance to their native Japan. This begged the question: is Pt. Reyes an orphaned piece of a larger landmass that broke apart? They theorized Japan might also have been part of this hypothetical lost continent."

"I'm liking what I hear so far, Professor," I said. "Is there anything else that makes Pt. Reyes unique?"

"Fault activity makes this area quite dynamic. It's a dangerous fault, and very active. The Pt. Reyes peninsula is essentially an island, moving imperceptibly north. If you consider variations of continental drift, and movements of the tectonic plates, Bolinas and the entire Peninsula it sits on should reach the Alaskan Trench within, oh, a million years."

"So, if this place isn't part of California, we're talking about an unknown continent?"

"It's possible," Pangloss said. "It could have been a small continent or a large island somewhere in the Pacific. This is all theoretical, of course, the theory being that our peninsula is from somewhere—out there." His hand swept toward Brighton Beach and the ocean beyond.

"Thanks, Dr. Pangloss," I said. "That's all I needed to know."

"This is all quite mysterious," the geologist said. "I can't imagine how it relates to Dr. Dvorak. But if I've helped you in some way, I'm happy."

The conversation turned to more personal matters. Isabelle gave Pangloss an abridged version of her life, starting with her graduation from Berkeley High, leaving out the juicier details, which, I assumed, were many. Two hours and a few shots of brandy later, we wished the geologist a Merry Christmas and were on our way back to civilization.

The trip from Bolinas to San Anselmo was uneventful. Isabelle fell asleep with her head on my shoulder. As long as she slept, there was no chance for more of her hanky panky, though a few salacious thoughts did cross my mind at a San Anselmo stop light.

Isabelle's Packard sat alone in the Seminary parking lot. The men in the blue Chrysler got tired of waiting and returned home to Herr Vedanta.

"Wake up, Isabelle! We're back."

"Umm, did I miss anything?"

"If you did, it's not worth remembering. Now get behind the wheel of your pretty yellow car and you'll be safe and sound in your palatial wigwam in no time."

She followed me through the Seminary grounds as far as Bolinas Avenue. I turned left for San Francisco; she turned right for Ross.

26
Found Out

San Francisco sits on seven hills, and on any given day I'm climbing one of them, especially the one to my Telegraph Hill apartment. It was 11:30 when I climbed the long flight of stairs to my cozy hovel. I found Professor Dvorak still awake, puffing on his briar. The sweet smell of pipe tobacco filled the room. He'd been reading a copy of *Thrilling Wonder Stories*, pulled from my collection.

I went straight to the liquor cabinet to mix a drink. Refresher in hand, I'd barely collapsed onto my overstuffed chair when the Prof began pumping me for news.

"How was Isabelle," he asked from the edge of his seat.

"She's doing fine," I soothed.

"And Eric Pangloss? How's he doing?"

"He seemed confused about my interest in Pt. Reyes geology, and what it has to do with your death," I said. "But he and Isabelle talked, and that made him happy."

I gave the Prof the same dope Pangloss gave me. There was enough circumstantial evidence to suspect Pt. Reyes was part of Vedanta's lost Lemuria, as he'd written in "Quo Valis."

A knock on the front door ended our conversation, but quick. Our eyes met in dead silence. The knock came again. I slipped my .38 from its holster, tiptoed to the door, and pressed my back to the wall.

"Who is it?"

"It's Isabelle Dvorak, Alex. Let me in!"

I exhaled and lowered my gun.

"The jig is up, Professor," I said. "It's your daughter."

I opened the door wide enough to give Isabelle Dvorak a clear view of her dear departed papa, seated in the chair behind me. Her pan drained of all color.

In confused disbelief she blurted out: "Father?"

At which point, her baby blues rolled back into their sockets and her lithesome body went as limp as a cooked noodle. The thick shoulder pads on her coat cushioned her fall.

I scooped her up and carried her inside, kicking the door closed behind me. I laid her on the sofa, at which point the Prof began fanning her pretty puss with *Thrilling Wonder Stories*. Then he stood up.

"I'll get some water!" he squawked. "Have you got any smelling salts?"

I held out a pony glass of Vat 69. "Give her this," I said.

He held it to her lips. She coughed. She sputtered. She frothed. Then she came to.

"How is this even possible?" she sobbed.

Then her salty optics fastened on me.

"Why didn't you tell me Father was alive, you, you, I don't know what you are!"

Dvorak intervened on my behalf. "I'm sorry, Belle," he said, "but I couldn't let Mr. Blade tell you. It was for your safety as well as mine. It was just too dangerous."

"Danger? That's all I hear about! Danger danger danger! What does it mean?!"

Then she turned back to me.

"You, you!" She spat like a feral cat. "I hate you, Alexander Blade!"

A silky voice put an end to the Dvorak damsel's vitriolic tantrum.

"It sounds like our little clubhouse has a new member," the voice said.

Isabelle swung a swivel on the Sky Room's number one showgirl, Paloma Liu Tsong, who had used her key to let herself in.

"Don't mind me," Paloma purred, sizing up the Dvorak canary. "I just dropped by to share the good news. The Chief says Little Pete the highbinder is history. He's been exorcised. The TV is still in a hundred pieces, but I don't smell sulfur and brimstone, either. The Chief chopped up the weejee board and burned it with some white sage. So, that's that."

"I'll bet he made himself real popular with the other tenants for that one," I said. "And the drumming."

"Oh, you bet. Dr. Painless called the fire department. When they showed up with their hoses and ladders and such, the Chief told them he was just exorcising an evil spirit. No big deal. In any case, Little Pete hasn't shown his ugly mug for two whole days."

"That's the best news I've heard all week," I whooped. "Now we can send the Chief back to his island paradise in Golden Gate Park!"

My jubilation was short-lived. The presence of the two females had dropped the room temperature below freezing. It was time to start with introductions.

"Paloma, this is the Professor's daughter, Isabelle. Isabelle, meet Paloma, my Girl Friday and future PI at Confidential Investigations."

They were two wolverines, sizing each other up. Paloma was the first to take a bite.

"You're much younger than Alex described you," she nipped. "I don't think you look anything like a schoolmarm, does she, Alex?"

"Well, ladies," I joked, "now that we're on a friendly, first name basis, let's get a handle on these new developments. There's a good possibility Miss Dvorak was followed, in which case, Freeps will stake out my digs and, *ipso facto*, they'll know the Professor lives here.

"If she wasn't followed, we're in luck, but we can't take that chance. Until we know which way the wind blows, I'll slip the Professor out the back door, back to his little hideaway on Ocean Beach."

"I'm sorry, Father," Isabelle said. "If I'd known you were in hiding, I never would have come here."

"It's not your fault, Belle. Mr. Blade is right. I'd better go. Dining on midway food isn't as bad as the alternative."

"Once you're safe, Professor, I'll find out what Vedanta's been up to. Snooping through his bunker is out; too many armed guards. I'd have a better shot at Shipwreck Cemetery. My contact at the Call-Bulletin says there's been Freep activity out there, but no one seems to know what they've been up to."

"Before you go, Blade, I suggest you purchase a Geiger counter to detect any radioactivity from your surroundings," Dvorak advised. "It's the only way you'll know when you're near plutonium."

27
Fans Will be Fans

I drove the Hudson west on Geary, into the Richmond district. Destination? Smilin' Sam's Army Navy Surplus. It was the only place in town that might sell a Geiger counter. My war surplus office furniture came from Smilin' Sam's. Now that the war is over, the government has boatloads of wartime bric-a-brac to unload, and that might include Geiger counters.

But first I dropped anchor at King's Koffee Kup, the diner next door to Smilin' Sam's on the corner of 19th and Geary. I'm a Koffee Kup regular. The owner has a photo of me behind the counter, a scene from my very first picture, "Baby Makes Three," with Ben Turpin. I was just a curtain climber when my movie career took off. Hell, I was still a kid when it ended.

Fans can get real nosey when they recognize me. The one question they want to know is, why did I quit Hollywood at the top of my game? They've come up with some doozeys on their own, like, did my voice change and I couldn't make it in the talkies? For me it was too personal, so I never explained.

My mother was my agent in those days. When she died in the accident, two things happened: my movie career hit the curb, and I became an orphan. That was when Uncle Jesse, the captain of San Francisco's famous Chinatown Squad, took me under his wing. Through the years, he taught me all I know about law enforcement. So, when I was old enough, I joined the San Francisco Police Department, just like him.

Then came that little kerfuffle with the Axis. So, I joined the Marines and got a free ticket to the South Sea Islands. The problem was, the Nips got their tickets to the same islands, and were hell bent on killing me. I'm still trying to figure out how they didn't manage that.

After the war, I could have tried to shoehorn my way back into Hollywood, but by then, I was no spring chicken. I didn't want to end up like the Bowery Boys, wearing beanie caps like middle-aged morons. Instead, I applied for my California PI's license and opened Confidential Investigations.

Sure, I'm no millionaire, but I call the shots. I choose my clients, and Paloma is the hottest babe in Chinatown.

"Snap out of it, Buster," King Blaylock said from behind the counter. King owned the Koffee Kup. He was a New Orleans expat who stayed in Frisco after the war. He had yellow, marcelled hair and a pencil mustache. His arms were long enough to reach the highest shelf behind the counter.

"You looked like you was a million miles away. Somethin' on your mind?"

"Maybe I'm just hungry, King. How about one of your Ocean Beach Benedicts?"

"You got it!" Blaylock turned to yell at Cap True, the cook.

"Ocean Beach Benedict, and make it snappy, Cap!"

While nursing my coffee, a dame with two kids sitting at a nearby table caught my eye. She was a full-figured touched-up blonde with very styled hair. Her chest bulged against the tailored gray suit she wore. Her flared jacket exaggerated full hips, and her gams displayed nicely under gunmetal sheers. She wore fire engine red lipstick and was laying the heavy hinge in my direction. Somehow she'd pegged me as the Wonder Boy of the Westerns.

When King put my Eggs Benedict on the counter, the frail made her move. She and her offspring, a boy and a girl—twins from the look of them—plopped her fulsome flanks on the stool next to mine. She apologized profusely for imposing on me, then proceeded to do so.

"I'm so sorry to intrude, but are you Buster Blade?"

"Wonder Boy of the Westerns, yes ma'am," I drawled.

"I thought so! I was your biggest fan when I was my daughter Kathy's age. I had the hugest crush on you in fourth grade! I can't tell you how many times you showed up in my diary!"

"Mommy, can we go now?" Kathy's brother whined.

"In a moment, Bud; Mommy's speaking with Mr. Blade."

My Benedict was getting cold, so I began stuffing my mug. Kathy piped up next.

"Mommy, I'm hungry. Can we get something to eat?"

"In a minute, Sweetie, Mommy's busy," the blonde soothed as she dug into her purse. She brought out a pen, but couldn't find a scrap of paper. She looked at King. "Sir? May I see a menu?"

King brought a menu, handed it to the blonde, who pushed it toward me with one hand while holding a pen in the other.

"Would you mind awfully if I asked for your autograph, Mr. Blade? I'd be forever grateful."

"Say, Lady," King broke in. "We charge a deposit on those menus. That'll be five cents if you're taking it home."

Miffed, the blonde reached back into her purse for a nickel and handed it to King, who dropped it into the till.

"Thank you kindly, ma'am," King said in an exaggerated Southern drawl.

Once upon a time I had no patience with fans like her. Now, so few bother me that, well, one little autograph couldn't hurt.

"Okay, what's your name, Missus…"?

"Just make it out to Norma," she replied coyly.

"To Norma, my biggest fan of all time, Love, Buster Blade, Wonder Boy of the Westerns. How's that?"

"Absolutely fabulous, thank you forever and ever," the curvaceous cutie replied. She glanced around to make sure King wasn't listening.

"Um, if you're ever in Redwood City," she whispered, "I'd love to return the favor. I'm in the phonebook under Norma Shearson."

Here we go again, I thought. It's that Tinsel Town mystique. Fans from time immemorial can't resist its magnetic pull.

I said: "You're too kind, Norma."

"MOMMY!"

Fan mom grabbed the squirt's arm and squeezed it, hard.

"Stop interrupting Mommy when she's talking to an adult! Santa will cross you off his list if you don't behave!"

Again she thanked me, then swiveled her hindquarters back to her table, children in tow. She plopped them in their chairs, admiring her newly autographed menu before giving her order to King. I thought I'd handled the situation well.

I pushed off my empty plate, laid two dollars on the counter, and said: "Keep the change. See you next time, King."

The buxom mommy with naughty thoughts flashed a smile as I ankled out the door. Yep, the old Hollywood allure. It's all about Hollywood.

• • •

Any day now, the jolly fat man would be sliding down the chimney. The aisles at Smilin' Sam's Army Navy Surplus were bustling with guys looking for parts to build their holiday projects, the kind of stuff you see in *Popular Mechanics*, like "How to Turn Your Crosley Station Wagon Into a Flying Car," stuff like that.

Smilin' Sam's was the go-to destination for exotic junk on the cheap, built for the war effort and made to last as long as we were in it. The gun counter was two rows thick in customers. Army handguns were on pre-Christmas sale. A gat would fit nicely in the little woman's Christmas stocking, but all I needed was a Geiger counter. Somehow, that seemed exotic.

Rummaging through the spent Howitzer shells, G.I. helmets, combat boots, and rubber gas masks, I found what I was looking for: an olive green box with a detector at the end of a two-foot cord. It was the last one. Now that the Reds were building their own atomic arsenal, these babies had become real popular.

The price was right, too; only $4.98, and all it needed was one "D" cell mercury battery, which I bought at the counter for ten cents. Hanging above the counter, a banner with big red letters said, "BETTER DEAD THAN RED."

28
Freeps are Creeps

I took my new Geiger counter to Telegraph Hill, parked the Hudson, then hopped a trolley to a rent-a-car agency on Van Ness Avenue, where I hired a nondescript, black Nash Airflyte sedan. I tossed the Geiger counter in the back seat and was barreling across the Golden Gate Bridge on the 101 heading north to Marin.

At Tomales Bay, Sir Francis Drake skirted the shoreline to Inverness, where I slowed to ten miles per hour through its one block business district. One mile farther down the road I passed Chicken Ranch Beach. From there, the road curved uphill to the left.

A fork in the road a few miles later gave me the choice of north or south. I went south, taking Old Lighthouse Road.

The Professor said I'd see a ship-to-shore radio outpost before I reached the marble orchard. Rows and rows of wooden poles, twenty feet high, stood out against the gray sky. The poles were part of a massive radio antenna that picked up signals from ships at sea. They were hard to miss.

From the Professor's description, the small knoll of eucalyptus trees dead ahead was Shipwreck Cemetery. With nary a soul in sight, I veered off the road onto a dirt siding that led to the graveyard.

December in these parts means plenty of wind and rain, and that had turned the dirt into mud, the kind that clings to shoes in thick clumps. I donned my raincoat and hat, grabbed the Geiger counter from the back seat, and exited the warmth of the car's interior.

I followed a well-used path through thistles and Queen Anne's Lace. At the end of the path, a gate swung eerily in the wind. The trees danced wildly above moss covered tombstones.

I counted a half dozen stones from where I stood. But that was just on this side of the knoll. I couldn't see the other side. Broken branches and dried eucalyptus leaves littered the gravesites. If Omenon had been here, I saw no evidence of it.

Another ten tombstones came into view as I crested the top of the knoll. Then rain began to fall. Small drops that got bigger and heavier fast. I was dressed for foul weather, but didn't have to like it.

Fallen branches and the dim light made it difficult to maneuver between the headstones on uneven ground. Then, one grave caught my eye. I snapped on my penlight and took a closer look. The headstone confirmed my suspicion that something wasn't right. Its unknown tenant perished when the ship *Clandestine* sank off Bolinas Lagoon on November 29, 1900, yet the dirt on the grave looked fresh.

I reached for the Geiger counter. Adjusting the meter to zero, I flicked the toggle switch to the ON position, unrolled the cord with the thingamabob on the end and swiped it over the grave. Bingo! The box began clicking like Grandma's false teeth. The dial on the meter bounced so hard I got nervous. I turned it off and backed away.

The trees moved wildly above the tombstones.

Then I noticed other piles of freshly dug earth on other graves. I turned on the click-box and swept it over a few more. CLICKITY CLICK CLICK! This was it! Ananda Vedanta's hidden stash of plutonium. I swirled the detector over another suspicious grave and got a different reading. This one was far less radioactive than the others, but still gave the needle a tweak.

I tore a loose picket from the surrounding fence, turned it into a makeshift shovel, and started digging. Two feet down, a metallic "clank" stopped my shoveling. Brushing dirt aside with my hands, I uncovered a foot-long metal cylinder. The Geiger counter blipped and clicked a few times, just enough to let me know this one was only slightly warm.

I put the cylinder to the side and replaced the dirt I'd removed from the grave. My ghoulish chore complete, I shined the penlight on my strap watch. It was edging on two o'clock. I had to get moving. It was still daylight, but you wouldn't know it. Dense rain clouds made the place gloomier, darker.

I returned to the path and was closing in on the Nash when I piped a pair of headlights coming my way, more than likely a dairy rancher returning home from Pt. Reyes Station. Then again, the car could be coming from the Omenon bunker.

I slid behind the wheel, kicked the starter, and bounced the Nash back onto Old Lighthouse Road. The distant car had picked up speed. It was closing in, and it was not a farm truck. As I sped past the oncoming Chrysler, five nasty-looking Freeps gave me the beady eye, and from the looks on their mugs they didn't like what they saw.

I checked my rear-vision mirror. The Chrysler was making a clumsy U-turn on the narrow road. I souped the Airflyte's cylinders with a shot of ethyl and it took off like an overweight jackrabbit.

The Nash, being a few pounds shy of a Sherman tank, leaned heavily into the turns. A Chrysler isn't exactly a sport car, and that evened things up. I wanted out of Marin County, far from the long arm of Omenon. But that was still miles away. With Freeps closing in, I decided to take a stand in Pt. Reyes Station. I'm rarely the optimistic type, but I had my .38 and enough lead to hold out until the cavalry arrived. The world was my oyster.

Christmas elves had not overlooked Pt. Reyes Station. I sped under festive garlands draped across the road, squealing to a stop in front of the Pt. Reyes Farmers Bank. Large red bows hung inside each of its two windows. The building looked substantial enough for a standoff, and I was sure the bank employees would call the sheriff as soon as lead began to fly. I kicked my car door open and made for the bank at full tilt.

Addressing the wide-eyed bank teller in her cage, I yelped: "There's a car full of armed bandits behind me and they're coming to heist your bank! Call the sheriff! I'll try to hold them off!"

The teller, last year's Miss Dairy Queen, wore a tailored business suit. A few short months ago, she had charted a new career path, from dairy farm to high finance. She hadn't planned on a bank heist, however, and didn't know what to make of me.

"I'll get the manager!" she yeeped, deserting her station in a flash.

Pt. Reyes Farmers Bank, being a small institution, had no security guard. I slammed the front doors, slid the lobby's flag pole through the door handles, and pulled down the shades as my pursuers screeched to a halt.

Freeps dressed in Omenon's regulation bib overalls and red long johns tumbled out of the Chrysler. They carried baseball bats, and they weren't looking for a third baseman. The driver, an Omenon group leader, did the talking.

"Come on out, Friend," the Freep menaced. "We know you're in there. We just want to talk."

I said, "You're outta luck, Friend! I've already signed with the Cubs. Go back to your Fuhrer."

"C'mon, man. Don't be such a Norm," he coaxed in a sympathetic tone. "We can wait all day if we have to. How about you?"

"Go ahead—talk," I said.

The commotion flushed the bank manager out of his office, where he had just dialed the sheriff. He had closed the hardened steel door to the safe, spun the lock, and ran to the dairymaid like a protective papa.

"I'll have you know I've called the s-sheriff," he announced.

"Good man," I barked. "That's what we need, the law!"

The Freeps had roused several locals from out of The Western Saloon. Freeps were not welcome in Pt. Reyes Station. The locals expected them to stay on their side of the mountain. Within minutes, locals outnumbered Freeps three to one.

An aggressive farm hand in a plaid wool jacket shoved one of the Freeps. The Freeps repositioned themselves back-to-back and threatened the crowd with their wooden weaponry. That did not go over well with the farmers. Beer cans and milk bottles rained down on the Freeps.

But Freeps are trained to go down fighting no matter how far outnumbered. Fists flew into faces. Blood splattered. The fight was on. A siren wailed in the distance. The Freeps heard it and recalculated their position. They chose a hasty retreat.

"Okay, Friend," the group leader yelled through the bank doors. "You win this round. We'll see you again. You can count on that."

They fought their way back to the Chrysler, and in a snarl of cylinders, made a sharp U-turn to beat a hasty retreat back to Inverness and the safety of the bunker. The siren was closing in.

I turned to the bank manager. "No need to thank me," I said. "And don't forget to tell the sheriff that Omenon tried to break into your vault!"

I dashed to the Airflyte, stomped the starter, and hightailed it back to the Big City.

29
It Came From Outer Space

The office smelled of white sage and copal incense and Paloma's beloved TV set was in a hundred pieces, but I didn't care. I had more important things to think about.

I slipped the metal cylinder from my coat pocket, placed it on top of my desk, and began wiping off graveyard mud with a page from last week's *Chronicle*. As I was thus engaged, from out of nowhere the Chief stood behind me, as if he had dropped through the skylight.

"Holy Mother of Pearl!" I squawked. "Don't sneak up on me like that, Chief!"

"Chief not sneak," he said matter-of-factly. "This normal walking for shaman. What trouble white man bring home now?" The Chief examined the cylinder. "This no ordinary tin can. Where you find it?"

"I dug it out of Shipwreck Cemetery on Lighthouse Road," I said. "Chief, this could be the smoking gun that'll nail Ananda Vedanta. If I'm right, this could land him in the clink but good."

The Chief wrinkled his weathered forehead.

"Got news for you," he said. "Smoking gun still loaded. Hokay, Chief give white eye advice. No charge. Put tin can back where you got it."

We stood motionless, staring at the metal cylinder for what seemed like hours. It didn't move. Nor did it change color or make ominous ticking sounds. It was time to find out what was inside.

"Look at this, Chief," I said. "There's a groove on one end of this thing. I bet if I slipped your tomahawk blade into the groove and turned it, I could unscrew it."

"Chief give last warning to stupid white eye. Something alive in this thing."

"You have a great imagination, Chief," I scoffed. "Do you see any air holes? Nothing can live without air."

"Here we go again," the Chief droned. "White eye stirring up trouble over something he know nothing about. Don't forget, when it come to spirit world, you one big dope."

"Warning duly noted, Chief. Now, let's have that tomahawk."

Begrudgingly, the Chief handed it over. I grasped the cylinder, inserted the tomahawk blade into the groove, and turned. The cap moved. A couple more turns and it had loosened enough to finish the job with my fingers. I laid the top on the desk next to the upright cylinder. We both leaned over to look inside.

"It's about time!" a voice as thin as Paloma's negligee squeaked.

"Did you say something, Chief?"

"Not Chief. Tin can speak. Don't say Chief not warn you!"

A few spindly legs appeared, then an unusually colorful spider climbed onto the lip of the cylinder.

"I have only myself to blame!" the spider gasped.

"Grandmother Thought Spider!" The Chief screeched. "Oh, sacred Thought Spider, who wove my people into being and led us through the four worlds—why you in tin can?"

"Finally!" the spider said. "Someone on this sorry planet appreciates me. It's a long story, red creature, but first, what have you got to eat? I'm famished."

30
The Confession

On Unktomia, the Thought Spider's home planet, flies do not exist. But as far as the Chief was concerned, flies were what a spider needs most. The shaman dashed to a sunny window, where two flies bounced against the glass pane. He stunned them with a bundle of white sage and laid them out before the spider, which sucked their juices dry in seconds.

As I watched the gruesome spectacle, the Chief explained: "My peoples' world was in darkness until Thought Spider wove web up to sky. That when ancient chief climb web and fetch sun. Bring down to Earth. Then, Thought Spider give us fire, teach my people how to weave. White eye have no idea what we owe Thought Spider."

"You'd better listen to him," the spider squeaked. "According to your legends, I can sing planets into being, and I even made you. I can walk on water, too."

Modesty was not one of the spider's personality traits. Its multi-colored body meant it was from the north, the Chief said. He claimed there were spiders of other colors, too, coming from the east, west, and south.

It didn't take long to dope out how the spider "talked." Its "voice" came as a sharp sound inside my head, like broken glass hitting the floor. It took awhile to get used to. As we watched, it dropped its former meal onto the floor.

"Bueno," the spider belched in something that sounded like Spanish. "You asked how I came to be inside this metal prison. I'm ashamed to admit that an Earth creature pulled a fast one on me. We Unktomians can read minds, especially ones as primitive as yours. It's a great defense against those who wish to do us harm. But this time, I was sucker-punched.

"The creature you call Ananda Vedanta, was cunning. He sent one of his brainwashed Freeps to do his dirty work; one whose brain was washed so well there was nothing for me to read. This mindless minion knocked me out of my web into this lead-lined cylinder. Even my high-speed penetration ray couldn't get through. It's been unsettling, to say the least."

The Chief's mug went two shades lighter on hearing this.

"Never mess with web," the Chief warned. "Spider medicine animal."

It seemed the Chief and the spider were strangely simpatico. Even stranger, the spider had information about Ananda Vedanta that I needed for my case. It looked like the Chief was still on the payroll. I needed him to commune with the spider, which was extremely chatty. Later we determined that fly juice had a euphoric, almost hallucinogenic effect on Unktomian Thought Spiders.

"Ask the spider its name," I prodded the Chief. But, before the Chief could open his yap, the spider replied, "My name is Sus sistinnako."

I smiled. "That's a mouthful."

"You find the name amusing, detective?" The spider sounded miffed. "It is not an uncommon name on our planet."

"You know I'm a private detective?"

"What part of 'Unktomians can read minds' don't you get?"

This was the most sarcastic spider I'd ever run into. It continued:

"When Ananda Vedanta was still writing dopey science fiction stories, he was called Franticek Drtikol ," the spider said.

Wobbling back and forth under the influence, the spider explained how it had a need for atomic fuel to power its ship. It also gave me the back-story on "Quo Valis" and "Skeets Malloy," Drtikol's most infamous sci-fi yarns.

"I wrote them," the spider confessed. "It didn't matter to me that Drtikol's name was on the byline. It was all part of my plan."

The spider's plan was bunk, if you ask me. For reasons beyond comprehension, it came up with the idea to use Drtikol as its proxy to write sci-fi yarns as a basis to found a religion. Then it put Franticek Drtikol in charge. Its ultimate goal was, of course, fuel for its ship.

"Things got ugly," the spider explained, "when Drtikol's success turned him into a megalomaniac. As Ananda Vedanta, he thought he was a conduit for universal power. His Freep followers worshipped him, and he grew narcissistic and paranoid.

"Then he turned on me," the spider rasped. "He figured I'd double cross him somehow. He made plans to dispose of me, but feared retribution for killing an Unktomian, so, I was simply relocated."

"That's quite a story," I said. "It even sounds like one of Drtikol's sci-fi yarns."

"What I give, I can take away," the spider proclaimed dreamily. "Meanwhile, I think I'll enjoy this place. It's got plenty of your Earth flies, and this red creature with bird feathers on his top understands me.

He says he disposed of a Deadbeat that was making whoopee with your female assistant."

I said: "You mean Little Pete was no ordinary evil spirit?"

"Wasn't that obvious?" the spider wheezed. "He was a Deadbeat from old Earth, trying to be a Comeback."

"I thought Deadbeats were a figment of Drtikol's pulp yarns."

The spider shrugged three of its legs.

"Like I said, 'Quo Valis' tells it like it is."

"It's a science fiction story," I countered.

"I beg to differ," the spider replied. "It's based on fact. I witnessed the events in the story, the whole package: Project Mind Fuhrer, the explosion, and the re-materialized Earth planet. I'm telling you that when the Nazis destroyed your Earth, billions of organic energy nodules, souls to you, went on the dole. They've been trying to make a comeback ever since. Thousands of them already have. They use Omenon-issued Ouija boards to breach the minds of clueless Norms. Your Chinese highbinder got here through a talking board, didn't he?"

"Now that you mention it, he did," I said. "I thought Ananda Vedanta used those boards to cleanse Deadbeats from his followers. At least, that's what he claims."

"Vedanta altered my plan," the tiny tarantula said. "He uses the boards to infect his followers, not cleanse them. His goal is to bring back as many Deadbeats as he can to do his bidding. He thinks he can raise Lemuria and claim it as his seat of power. My plan was to take the plutonium away from him before he got to the bomb-making stage. Then, I'd give him the heave-ho."

31
The Bum's Rush

Like it or not, the annoying arachnid was my new partner. The Chief and the spider were on the same wavelength, which meant the shaman stayed on the payroll to keep me apprised of the spider's shenanigans.

You'd think Nazi A-Bombs set to blow the tripes out of California would be enough to interest the Feds. If Leroy St. James threw his weight behind this case, the G-men should sit up and take notice.

And so, I flagged my brogans back to police headquarters, hoping St. James had recovered from his failed affair with Gene Tierney. I found the self-proclaimed world's greatest detective at his desk, counting thumbtacks he'd dropped on the floor.

"Sorry to barge in on you without prior notice, Lieutenant, but this is urgent."

"Dammit, Blade! You made me lose count! Now I'll have to start over. One, two..."

"Okay, but before you do, hear me out. The lives of countless citizens hang in the balance."

I gave St. James the whole ball of wax about Omenon's plan to revive Hitler's Project Mind Fuhrer using Nazi scientists. I even told him about the space spider that created this mess. When I stopped talking, an awkward silence filled the room. St. James's normally white cheeks turned florid pink.

Uncomfortably, I continued: "I realize this is hard to swallow, Lieutenant. If I hadn't talked to the spider myself, I wouldn't bother you. But if you back me up it will be hard for the Feds to ignore this national threat."

I waited. It looked as though he was thinking hard about what I'd just said, but the strained look on his sour puss was indigestion. He went to his desk drawer, pulled out a Dixie cup, filled it with Bromo-Seltzer, and downed it in one gulp.

"Blade, I won't beat my gums to death over this," he began in a holier-than-thou tone. "I always knew Hollywood would catch up with you. Everyone knows ex-movie brats have problems, but yours are in a class by themselves.

"Wake up, Buster! It's as plain as the nose on your face. You long for the days when you rode the range with Tom Mix and Fuzzy Coots, and you've been looking for something to take their place ever since. For a time, you had a promising career with the SFPD. But you ditched that to become a private snoop. Apparently, even that wasn't enough.

"Now you're Flash Gordon, locking sabers with Ming the Merciless. You see little green spiders writing science fiction stories on tiny typewriters for eight hands. And the stories are true!

"You're right about one thing, though. I have a reputation, and a damn good one. That means I wouldn't go out on a limb for this wild hare on a bet! It would ruin me worse than it has you! Now, go get help from one of those Hollywood headshrinkers before I slap you in the 'gow for annoying an officer of the law!"

32
Find Buster Blade!

Behind his desk of polished whale skull, Ananda Vedanta demanded to know why Project Mind Fuhrer was behind schedule. Galactic Rangers had already scouted the detonation sites. What was the holdup? Vedanta was on the verge of an Ex-Lax Energizer when Project Mind Fuhrer's lead scientist, Regis Toomey, entered Vedanta's inner sanctum on Christmas Eve.

Vedanta's angry stare played an accordion solo up and down Toomey's spine.

"Yah, Mind Fuhrer?" he squeaked.

"Toomey, I grow impatient. Project Mind Fuhrer has not yet reached completion," Vedanta growled. "I need those bombs! What's the problem?"

"We want to be absolutely certain we don't repeat the mistake we made five years ago," Toomey sputtered. "We destroyed the world once, and could do it again. And if we do, we can't be sure there will be another Earth to take its place."

Vedanta glanced at the map on his desk. He picked up his pack of Lucky Strikes, slipped one out, and lit it. He exhaled and—changed the subject.

"Someone has been snooping around the cemetery. A Freep scout unit chased him but he got away. If he's stolen any of our property, it could put Project Mind Fuhrer in jeopardy. That's why I need those Sun Bombs now, toot sweet, Toomey!" Vedanta pounded the whale skull with both fists. "*Understand?*"

Toomey's nerves were unraveling. "Y-yah, I under-s-stand, Mind Fuhrer." He with pulled a handkerchief from his lab coat and wiped beads of sweat off his forehead. "We'll put a rush on it, but it could be dangerous."

This only annoyed Vedanta further. He clenched his grinders and barked, "Enough! You nearly succeeded in 1945! Since then you've had plenty of time to perfect it. Get to it! Chop chop!"

"Yah, Mind Fuhrer!"

Toomey beat a welcome retreat to his laboratory on Level 1. Still fuming, Vedanta flicked on his intercom and said: "Tell Robert Armstrong I want to see him, now!"

No one seemed to know why Vedanta named the members of his inner circle after B movie character actors. Robert Armstrong was chief of security. Yes, that Robert Armstrong, the guy who starred with Fay Wray in King Kong. A few short years ago in Nazi Germany, Armstrong was Bramhag Dohrn, feared Gestapo colonel.

"Yah, Mind Fuhrer?" Dohrn screeched, clicking his heels for added effect. Dohrn had the pallid features of Bela Lugosi, but was taller and heavier. His hair had a center part, which was all the rage after Hitler's Putsch. He wore a Darhoff gabardine suit by Botany 500 that must have set him back a cool sixty bucks.

"Listen, Armstrong," Vedanta barked, "we have a leak in the dam. It's the kind of leak that needs to be plugged with lead. Got it? This particular leak has been snooping around the cemetery. I want you to find out who the leak was and stop it. Somehow, this eluded my Galactic Rangers, and I don't want that to happen again, understand?"

"Yah, Mind Fuhrer!"

"Our leak was last seen at the Pt. Reyes Farmers Bank. Start there. Now go!"

"Yah, Mind Fuhrer!"

Dohrn clicked his heels, spun around, and marched out the door to downtown Inverness.

• • •

Stopping for a pack of cigarettes at the Inverness General Store, Bamhag Dohrn saved himself a trip to the Pt. Reyes Farmers Bank when he purchased the latest edition of the *Pt. Reyes Gazette*. Not much happens in Pt. Reyes Station, but when it does, it makes front-page news. In bold, black letters above the fold, the headline read: "Riot at Farmers Bank! Sheriff Seeks Freeps for Questioning."

Dohrn's next stop was the sheriff's office. If the sheriff wanted to speak with the Freeps that were involved in the bank altercation, Dohrn would make himself accessible, even subservient.

"Naturally, Sheriff," Dohrn guffawed with a slight lisp behind his German accent, "Omenon welcomes your investigation. I'll see to it these men are in your office this afternoon. I also read in the *Gazette* there was a private detective involved?"

The sheriff coughed through his cigar smoke. "That's right," he choked. "A citizen got his license number before he fled the scene. The car belongs to Van Ness Auto Rentals of San Francisco. All we want is a statement from the driver. It appears it wasn't a bank robbery like we thought, just an altercation between locals and your Omenon members. The most we can get out of this is a disturbing the peace rap, unless someone files assault charges. I've put my deputy on the case."

"There will be no charges coming from Omenon, Sheriff," Dohrn said, his eyelids drooping lazily. "I'm sure we can come to an agreeable solution on this, shall we say, unfortunate event. Thank you for your cooperation."

Dohrn hustled outside to his Chrysler. A glazed-eyed Freep sat stoically behind the wheel.

"Take me to Van Ness Auto Rentals in San Francisco. But first, pull up to that phone booth at the service station. I'll need the address from the phone book."

The attendant at Van Ness Auto Rentals wasn't keen on doling out company information to Dohrn and his Freep driver. Not until Dohrn flashed a $20 bill.

"Yes, here it is," the attendant said, referring to his rental log. "It was a Nash Airflyte sedan, black, rented to a Mr. A. Blade, suite 42, Mayfair Building."

Before you could warble *Deutschland Uber Alles*, the Holy One's Gestapo had me dead to rights as Fu Chan's private richard, the same private richard that defiled their cemetery and knew Isabelle Dvorak. Dohrn didn't waste time. His Unwelcome Wagon was standing at the door of Confidential Investigations, reading Paloma's "Closed for the Holidays" sign made out of holly and pipe cleaners. As festive as the sign was, it put Bramhag Dohrn in a foul mood.

"*Kommen du, Freep!*" he ordered. "Blade will return, and when he does…"

You've seen enough of those movie serials to finish that sentence. I've seen my share, too, which is why I knew Ananda Vedanta's next move would come straight out of Chapter Six.

33
Kidnapped

After my failed pitch to St. James, I rethought my options. I put the word out for everyone to meet me at the Black Cat on Montgomery Street. Paloma, Chief Iron Lung, and the Chief's ten-legged space thing assembled at the appointed time.

The usual Bohemian refugees were there, too: the Socialists, free speech advocates, flying saucer buffs, naturists, vegetarians, and plainclothes FBI agents.

Unlike the rest of us, the spider didn't need a chair. It hung from a thin strand of synthetic fiber attached to a potted plant. Its mode of

transportation was the Chief's hatband, where a large wrinkle offered enough space for the spider to fit inside.

"Okay, attention, everyone," I grated, "the only two parties not in attendance are Stan Raycraft and Isabelle Dvorak. Of those two, the Dvorak dame is the most likely to be in some kind of trouble. She should have been here by now."

That didn't bother Paloma, and the Chief was too busy sipping espresso and watching North Beach locals to care.

"As things stand," I said, "we're walking undertaker bait, just waiting for our mahogany overcoats. Ananda Vedanta's got our office staked out, and my apartment stash, too. He's hot on our trail."

After wrapping up my dire warning to the assembled trio, the counter clerk walked up to our table.

"You Mr. Blade?" he queried.

"That's right."

"This is for you." He laid a small envelope on the table. The envelope had my name on it, written with Germanic flourishes. Without further explanation, the clerk retreated to his coffee grinder.

I tore open the envelope. *"Mr. Blade,"* the note began. *"Miss Dvorak is our guest. If you are concerned for her welfare, meet me at Fisherman's Grotto tonight at five o'clock. I will be upstairs in the booth closest to the bar."*

• • •

At five o'clock I walked to the prearranged booth inside Fisherman's Grotto. An ugly blister sat smoldering in the booth. He made Eric von Stroheim look like a choirboy.

Bramhag Dohrn, aka Robert Armstrong, sat alone, daintily puffing a gasper on the end of a sterling silver cigarette holder. He was the kind of Nazi straight out of a matinee thriller, with the black suit, the pasty mug, the ice blue eyes, and Brilliantined hair combed straight back with a pitchfork. A few short years ago we were sending these fifth column creeps to San Quentin. But the war's over now, and they come and go as they please. I sauntered up and introduced myself.

"Is this seat taken, or are you saving it for der Fuhrer's second coming?"

"Amusing, Mr. Blade. Do sit down. Would you care for a drink?"

"Normally, I would say yes, but in this case, I'd rather not drink the arsenic you've got hidden in that signet ring you're wearing."

"Very well, have it your way, Mr. Blade. Let us get down to brass tacks, as you Norms like to say."

"If, by Norms, you mean red-blooded, tax-paying, overworked Americans, then yes, let's. What's all this chatter about Isabelle Dvorak?"

"It has come to my attention that you have information that only an Omenon insider would have. Furthermore, your employment by Dr. Dvorak's, or should I say, 'Lester Brannon's' manservant leads me to believe that the good doctor may not have perished in his automobile accident after all. The point is, Mr. Blade, Dvorak is alive, and you know where he is."

"You're jumping to conclusions, Fritz. Let me jump to one myself. Your pack of homicidal disciples bashed Fu Chan's steeple."

"You have a wild imagination, Mr. Blade." The lying Nazi ground his spent gasper in a plate of fried mozzarella sticks that had gone cold.

"Yeah, and it gets even wilder," I nudged. "You were hoping Fu Chan would rat out the Professor, but when he dug in his heels the Freeps cooked his oyster."

"This conversation is getting us nowhere, Mr. Blade! We know Dvorak is alive. I am sure he would want to know that his daughter is staying with his church. A church, I might add, that he callously abandoned. However, all is not lost. Our saintly leader wishes to forgive him and take him back."

"I'll bet he would. IF Dvorak were still alive."

"Stop playing games, Mr. Blade. Tell the Professor that his daughter is, as we speak, being groomed for her initiation into the Mind Fuhrer's breast pump brigade for nursing *kinder*. Do you know what must happen before a female secretes breast milk, Mr. Blade?"

"I took Physical Hygiene in high school, if that's what you mean."

"I'll accept that as a yes. When the Professor returns to Omenon, Ananda Vedanta will reconsider Miss Dvorak's assignment."

I rasped: "Never let it be said you Nazis don't know how to fight dirty."

"Your inner Deadbeat has made you extremely judgmental, Mr. Blade. Omenon can help you with that, if you give it a chance. You have 48 hours to return the Professor to our Inverness headquarters. I'm sure you know how to find us. You've already found our cemetery."

"Hold on, Heine," I yodeled. "I need to make a phone call." I waved a waiter over to our booth and asked for a telephone. He brought one, placing it on the table in front of me. I dialed Mai Ling at the Dvorak mansion. She picked up on the second ring.

"This is Alexander Blade talking. May I speak with Miss Dvorak?"

The high-pitched screech that came through the wire nearly split my eardrum.

"Miss Dvorak not come home!" Mai Ling squawked. "Gone all night. Me very worried. You find! You find!"

"Okay, I find, I find," I said, returning the phone to the waiter.

I was ready to wring the Nazi's neck, then put a slug through his Aryan clockworks. But that wouldn't bring back the Dvorak frail. In my mind's eye I saw her firm, perky glands being prepped for the dairy farm. This Gestapo geezer may have known Dvorak was alive, but he didn't know where he was. All I had to do was come up with a plan, and pronto.

34
The Sun Bomb

Deep in his underground laboratory, Regis Toomey chain-smoked his fifth coffin nail as he recovered from the tense meeting with his angry guru. He knew what Vedanta was capable of, and it could be far worse than an Ex-Lax Energizer.

Watching him closely was Toomey's new assistant, Heermark Graf, second in command at Project Mind Fuhrer. Vedanta had replaced Grundig Blaupunkt with Graf after Blaupunkt's recent treachery.

He was caught passing cult secrets to Sarah Surefire, a reporter at the *Pt. Reyes Gazette*. Surefire was writing an investigative series of articles about Omenon, her latest installment was about Vedanta's apocalyptic vision for the future.

Omenon rules strictly forbade contact with the press. An infraction meant serious consequences. Although Blaupunkt and Surefire were as secretive as a pair of love struck teenagers, Vedanta's spies were everywhere.

The All-Knowing Ones, a subsidiary of the Galactic Rangers, was the official name of Omenon's Gestapo unit. It was the AKO that uncovered Blaupunkt's traitorous behavior. Surefire knew something was wrong when Blaupunkt failed to show for their usual mail drop at the Western Saloon in Pt. Reyes Station.

Every Tuesday Blaupunkt would drive into town for supplies. After fulfilling his shopping list, he'd stop at the Western for a double Manhattan. While sitting at the bar, he scribbled notes to Surefire on a napkin. Surefire was there, too, but at the far end of the bar, nursing a martini. When Blaupunkt finished his drink, he'd crumple the napkin into his palm and drop it into the wastebasket near the front door. Surefire would down her martini and retrieve the note. The plan worked well until they were found out.

The following day, Surefire went to her mailbox to retrieve the morning mail. Instead of the usual Christmas card, she pulled out a rattlesnake clamped onto her wrist. Someone had removed the snake's rattle and turned it into a silent killer. The plucky reporter killed the snake with a nearby rock and ran to her phone for help before she passed out. The snake message was clear: stay away from Omenon, or die.

Blaupunkt's fate was a lesson to anyone who worked on Project Mind Fuhrer—do not talk to Norms. Still, lingering doubts kept some Omenon scientists awake at night, even Graf.

"But Herr Toomey," Graf said nervously. "I am not yet convinced of the stability of the Sun Bomb's exponential output. The Holy One says we destroyed our planet when we detonated the first Sun Bomb in 1945. Strangely, I have no memory of it. I only know what is written in Omenon doctrine. And yet, I am not convinced of Ananda Vedanta's conclusions."

"I know, I know," Toomey replied angrily. "But we have no choice in this matter. The Mind Fuhrer gets what the Mind Fuhrer wants. We will make his deadline and detonate all eight bombs as directed."

"When is the appointed hour?" Graf asked.

"You will find out when the time comes, Graf. Now, get back to work. We have five more bombs to assemble and we haven't much time."

Raising a mythical continent from the ocean floor was no simple task. It would take imagination and detailed planning. A diver had already placed a completed bomb on the San Andreas Fault in Tomales Bay. From there, the fault passed through the town of Olema, down the coast to the Bay Area and beyond. Vedanta, however, was interested only in the section under Tomales Bay, where the fault formed a schism between the Pt. Reyes peninsula and the rest of California.

The plan was to separate Pt. Reyes from the mainland as Lemuria rose. Vedanta's henchmen would place the other bombs according to his survey map. In theory, the impact from the Sun Bombs would shock the tectonic plate, releasing Lemuria from its underwater tomb. Pt. Reyes would then reconnect with its Lemurian sister.

The rest of the plan was simple. Vedanta would plunder the ancient Lemurian technology. As stated in "Quo Valis," the Lemurians had hermetically sealed their machines in caverns before the island went down.

35

Professor, Meet Thought Spider

The Hudson's windshield wipers valiantly fought a steady rain that pummeled the car. To make sure I wasn't being followed, I drove through the Embarcadero, Chinatown, and Golden Gate Park before reaching the amusement park at Ocean Beach. The rain hadn't slowed crowds of holiday pleasure seekers. At the Cabrillo Street Terminal, a flood of passengers surged from a B Line streetcar, heading to the Fun House.

Turning onto South Drive in Golden Gate Park, I pulled up to the windmill cottage. The Professor had no car and knew he was a hunted man. He'd be home. I tried not to spook him when I knocked on the weathered front door of the cottage.

"Professor? It's me, Blade! I have news!"

A face with the familiar Kaywoodie clenched in its teeth appeared behind a cracked windowpane in the door.

"Blade? What is it? What's the matter?" the Prof gasped as he opened the door on salt-rusted hinges.

"We've been found out," I said. "They've got Isabelle."

"What!?"

"It's extortion. You're the one they want, but she's the bait. I got it straight from Vedanta's Gestapo. They've figured out you're not dead. You've got to go back."

The Prof sighed. "I know enough about Vedanta's methods not to disobey. Even if we called the police, he has that bunker fortified. It could take weeks, even months, to flush him out. No telling what would happen to Isabelle."

"Don't fret, Professor. There've been some new developments. We've got an ace up our sleeve. I'll bring you up to speed on the way to town."

The Prof had brought so little with him we were on the road in no time. While we drove back, I gave him the lowdown on the cemetery, and the way the Geiger counter went haywire over the gravesites. He had some misgivings when I brought up the spider, but when I said the

Chief had given the spider an A-plus rating, he decided to set aside his doubts until he saw the spider for himself.

I planned to return the Prof on my terms, not Vedanta's, so I'd arranged to take him to a secret location—Andy Wong's Sky Room in Chinatown. Once we got there, we slipped through the backstage door. The floorshow as in full swing, featuring some of the sweetest Chinese showgirls in Frisco. They performed au natural, that is, if you ignored the pasties and nude thongs they wore.

Dvorak soaked this up like a biscuit in hot gravy. He toyed with the idea of a sociological study of Chinatown showgirls as we passed a room full of half-naked quails in the midst of a costume change. Gently, I guided him beyond to a nearby storage room where the Chief waited for us among racks of costumes and steamer trunks.

Dvorak had not seen Joe Iron Lung since his trip to the Chief's Humboldt County village in 1947. The two men exchanged a hearty handshake.

"Long time no see wise white eye from Cal Berkeley," the Chief greeted.

"It's wonderful to see you, too, Chief. But tell me, what's all this about a Thought Spider? Are you telling me Blade's wild story is true?"

At that, the Chief removed his top hat with the spider tucked in the headband. The spider hopped onto a crystal ball on an upright barrel that stood next to the Chief.

"Chief introduce Professor to Thought Spider in flesh," the Chief smiled. "This Professor Dvorak, Grandmother Thought Spider. He one smart cookie, and a paying customer, too."

Thought Spider undulated on top of the crystal ball. I wasn't sure what this behavior meant, other than it may have been hallucinating. Up and down, down and up, on and on it went.

"Greetings, Dr. Dvorak," Thought Spider finally said, or rather, thought. "May I call you Doctor?"

"Good heavens! It speaks!" the Professor yeeped. "Why, yes, that would be fine. I must confess, I find this experience somewhat disconcerting. It feels like I'm hearing your voice inside my mind, not through my ears."

"Very observant, Professor. I have no, as you call them, vocal cords. We Unktomians communicate through our etheric bodies. This transcends the process of waveform vocalization you call language. You can understand me despite your linguistic peculiarities. I can project my thoughts directly into your sentient nerve center. That's how you can understand me, even though I do not speak Earth language."

The Chief grinned. "Hot stuff, huh, Professor? No need for talking board when you got Thought Spider."

I wondered if the spider would be this chatty had it not been hopped up on fly juice. Whenever it felt the slightest hunger pang, the Chief was Johnny-on-the-spot with another fly. He had already used up the few flies at the office, and began smearing honey on the windowsills to attract more. I had no way of knowing if the spider's reasoning was compromised.

The Professor still looked shocked. A talking spider was difficult for a Berkeley professor to accept.

I said: "When I met the spider for the first time, I was like you are now, Professor. I thought I was delirious, losing my mind. Not that I can confirm it, mind you, but the Chief says these spiders helped his tribe out of a jam during the last ice age. They worshipped them; saw them as benevolent demi-gods."

"Yes," the spider interrupted. "Unktomians have a long history of interfering with the problems of lower life forms, helping them when they need it most. But I got carried away with Franticek Drtikol. All I needed was fuel for my ship. Instead, I saved Drtikol's dismal career, wrote his pulp stories for him, and turned him into a half-baked prophet.

"I suppose it was the drama, the angst," the spider coughed. "It's too easy to distract oneself on this planet, to lose track of one's purpose here. I've wasted far too much time already.

"However," Thought Spider continued, "what I wrote in 'Quo Valis' is true. This is not the same planet it was before your so-called Nazis destroyed it. However, I created Ananda Vedanta, and I can un-create him. He has defiled the power I gave him. I'll make things right again, with a little help from you."

"Fine," I said. "But this is where the Prof will stay until we make the swap. Meanwhile, we need to return to my inner sanctum to think this out."

36
The Master Plan

Sarah Surefire drifted in and out her delirium as she fought the snake venom. Sarah had a Plan B in case anything should happen to her. Stan Raycraft of the *San Francisco Call-Bulletin* agreed early on to be her backup.

When the delirium eased up, Sarah called Stan from her hospital phone.

"Stan? Sarah. Something's going on in Pt. Reyes, something big and it has to do with Omenon. Grundig Blaupunkt vanished without a trace before he could give me the scoop. Just so you know, I'm calling from San Rafael General Hospital. Omenon tried to kill me."

"Stan," Sarah pleaded, "you've got to take over for me. Go to the *Pt. Reyes Gazette*. My notes on Omenon are in the top drawer of my desk. I told the editor to let you have them. This can't wait."

Stan hung up the phone and turned to his friend and confidant: a bottle of Old Ripper. Don't ask me why, but that's when Stan remembered what I'd asked him at Sam Woo's the other night: "Tell me all you know about Ananda Vedanta," I'd said.

Stan rightly concluded my sudden interest in Vedanta and Surefire's attempted murder were not just coincidence. His reporter's brain shifted gears. When the editor looked the other way, he drained his bottle of Old Ripper, grabbed the phone, and dialed my number. Paloma picked up.

"Hi, Beautiful!" Stan chirped. "What time did you say our dinner date was?"

"I didn't," Paloma said. "What's up, Stanley? And no, Alex isn't here."

"Fine with me! We'll have the office all to ourselves."

"The Chief is here."

"Oh. In that case, I'll drop by and wait for Buster."

"Suit yourself. Alex should be here any minute."

"See you shortly, Delicious."

"You are too cute for words, Stanley." Click.

Raycraft grabbed a cookie that looked like a snowman from the communal party tray. He bit off the snowman's top hat, and headed out the door to Market Street, where he hopped a streetcar to the Mayfair Building. The sleigh bells on our office door jingled as he entered. Paloma had found them in the waste basket where I tossed them and put them back on.

"Huzzah, Gadzooks, and Merry Christmas to one and all!" Raycraft caterwauled in high spirits. "Where to the wassail bowl?"

I had just returned to the office before Stan arrived, and had settled into my inner sanctum. "There's no punch bowl, Stan" I said, strolling into the reception room, "but I have a bottle of Vat 69 in my desk drawer, if that meets your requirement for wassail."

"What? You keep that poor bottle in a drawer at this holiest time of year? Let it go and be fruitful! Make with the libations! It's almost Christmas!"

So, we made with the libations. Stan was soaring to the North Pole, plastered all the way. After reciting a few risqué Santa jokes, he got to the point of his visit.

"By the way," Stan slipped in casually, "what's up with you and Omenon, man?"

"What kind of question is that?"

"It's a straightforward question, Big Daddy and strictly legit," Stan replied. "It means what do you and Omenon have in common? I have solid reasons for making such an inquiry, sir. A fellow reporter and partner of mine, Sarah Surefire of the Pt. Reyes Gazette, was damn near killed by her mailbox! I mean, something inside her mailbox. Instead of Christmas ads, someone sent her a poisonous snake that chomped her flipper and curdled her innards. She's in San Rafael General as we speak."

Stan was working himself into such a snit, it caught Paloma's and the Chief's attention.

"We'd been working on a story together, see, about Omenon and what's going on behind the curtain in Pt. Reyes," Stan prattled. "Her source was about to name names. Something big was going to happen, she said, and soon. Maybe even before the New Year. What do you say, Buster? Shall we compare notes? I've got her files in my hot little hand. Let's down a thimbleful and seal the deal. Say, what's the Chief still doing here?"

"Who knows?" Paloma replied. "Maybe he likes it better here than his digs in the park."

The Chief gave them an upper plate dentist's grin.

"Hey!" Paloma yelped. "The Chief's got new teeth!"

The Chief beamed: "Painless Parker Christmas Special. Pay with dead presidents Chief get from white eye detective. Easy deal. Dentist just down hall."

"That's swell, Chief," I droned. "But we have more important things afoot than your new choppers. Omenon's got Isabelle Dvorak, and it has been strongly hinted they'll turn her into a sex slave if we don't turn over the Professor."

"Was that her idea or Omenon's?" Paloma sniped.

We were diverted from this catty display of femininity when a tiny screech filled our minds. It came from the spider.

"Has everyone forgotten I'm here, or do you ignore Unktomians because we couldn't care less about Christmas?" The spider had changed color from variegated green to a vibrant pink. The Chief's leathery mug looked concerned.

"Thought Spider plenty ticked off," the Chief said.

He explained that a Thought Spider has only two emotions: boredom and anger. Sandwiched between the two are an infinite number of interpretations.

"Maybe you should ask me about Vedanta's plan," the spider suggested. "I know what it is."

Stan was weaving, but still standing. He'd never seen a spider from outer space before.

"I t-think I'm having auditory hallucinations," Stan confessed. "Maybe I imbibed a trifle too much Christmas cheer today."

"You Earthmen lead such provincial lives," the spider sniffed. "I take it you've never met an Unktomian?"

Stan looked closer. The spider perched atop the metal canister on Paloma's desk. The Chief, being the spider's self-appointed liaison, introduced Stan.

"White eye reporter, meet Thought Spider," the Chief said. "She brought our people out of darkness into upper world many moons ago. Thought Spider knows all, sees all. Can help crazy white eyes, too, like she did my people. Speaks through mind, not ear flaps. Get it?"

"How many s-spiders are we talking about?" Stan slurred, vaguely speaking to the spider. "One, two? Hey, how'd you get here, talking spider?"

"On an interstellar spaceship, Inebriated One. I've been hoping to refuel it ever since I got here. Sad to say, I got sidetracked creating a minor religion for your people. Its prophet got too big for his britches and gave me the boot."

"You don't mean Ananda Vedanta!" Stan said, covering his mouth with his hand.

"That is exactly who I mean," the spider shot back. "If it weren't for the Earthman with the neatly trimmed hair feature above his nourishment orifice," it said, pointing a leg in my direction, "I would still be a prisoner in this cylinder. However, my incarceration gave me plenty of time to think."

"Wow, you are one crazy spider," Stan slurred. "An exclusive interview with a t-talking c-critter from outer space would put me in the Reporter's Hall of F-Fame. If you know Ananda Vedanta's big plan, let's hear it, man."

"I am not a man, and it's not *his* plan," the spider corrected. "I wrote it into my 'Quo Valis' trilogy, though he made a few changes here and there. We have more important things to talk about, like how to send Drtikol back to the desert bungalow where he belongs and I take his plutonium. If I hadn't been stuck inside this can, I would have taken from him long ago, and been on my way."

I let the spider have its hissy fit, but this was going nowhere fast. So, I came up with my own plan.

"Look," I said, lighting another gasper, "I've got to take the Prof to the bunker anyway, right? Your boy, Ananda, is expecting him. The Prof would be a perfect Trojan horse to get the spider inside the compound. Just climb aboard and keep its clam shut."

"Trojan horse?" the spider mused as it read my mind. "I see! It will appear as though it's just you and the Professor. Once we are inside the bunker, Drtikol will be mine."

• • •

Originally, Paloma and I had planned a cozy Christmas Eve in my apartment stash—that is, just the two of us. Somewhere along the line our plan got sidetracked. I had to take the Prof back to Omenon anyway, so we had nothing to lose by returning him to Telegraph Hill. The Chief had nowhere else to go, and neither did Stan, who had finished a tour of newsroom parties before showing up at my front door. He brought a half empty bottle of booze and a goofy grin.

"The grapevine says this is where the party's at, man!" Stan said to Paloma at the front door. She let him in.

The Chief was here and that meant Thought Spider was here, too. Spider was trying to dope out the Christmas angle of our gathering. Dr. Dvorak, being a professor, tried to fill in the gaps so the spider understood.

"What we call Christmas was once a winter celebration called Saturnalia," the egghead began. "It coincided with the shortest day of our planet's orbit around the sun. Tree worship was a feature of this winter celebration. Our so-called Christmas tree came from those ancient times. Later it became connected with the birthday of a Jewish carpenter who claimed to be the Creator itself."

The spider said: "And Earth creatures accept this story without question?"

"Well, many do, not all," the Professor replied. "Others have their own religious festivals that have nothing to do with the divine carpenter."

"And what of these colorful cubes, tied with webs," the spider said. "Where do they fit into this festival?"

The Chief cut in before the Professor could answer.

"White eyes call them Christmas presents," the Chief interrupted. "Sold by fat cat capitalist white eyes for exploitation of masses. All-knowing carpenter see both future and past at same time. Knew all about Santa, presents, after Christmas sales, and how his birthday exploit working classes to make rich capitalist richer."

"Thanks for the warm and fuzzy critique, Chief!" Paloma grouched as she handed out the gifts. "There's nothing I like better than hearing about the exploitation of the masses at Christmas."

The Professor turned to me and asked, "You know, I haven't heard from Fu Chan all week, Mr. Blade. I seem to have lost track of him, what with my nomadic lifestyle. Why isn't he here?"

I hated to be the bearer of bad news, but I told him. After that, the Prof clammed up and didn't say another word for the rest of the day.

We were less than 24 hours away from the Gestapo geezer's deadline to turn over the Professor. I had to get organized while we were all in one place. My plan included the Professor, the spider, and me.

Paloma couldn't be part of the team. Vedanta's guards wouldn't let her in anyway. The Chief wasn't included for the same reason. They'd remain at the office and wait to hear from me. If I didn't call them by midnight, they'd flag Leroy St. James. If we succeeded, I'd drop Fu Chain's killer in St. James's lap.

37
Cell Mates

Isabelle Dvorak squirmed uncomfortably on the mattress in a Level 3 holding cell. She stared at her size seven pumps. They were new when she arrived. Now they looked like she felt: scuffed and grimy.

She wasn't alone. Grundig Blaupunkt sat glumly in the cell opposite hers, smoking his daily ration of Camel cigarettes. Omenon's Galactic Prison Guard had sole authority to dispense *sigaretten*, that's Kraut for gaspers. The guards were a stingy lot, too, allowing only one cig per incarcerated customer per day.

Blaupunkt was confused by Isabelle Dvorak's presence. She wasn't a Freep, or any part of the temple's internal bureaucracy.

"Begging your pardon, *fraulein*," Blaupunkt said politely. "Allow me to introduce myself. I am Dr. Grundig Blaupunkt, formerly second in command of Project Mind Fuhrer. As you can see, I am currently unemployed. May I ask what brings you here? You do not look like a threat to Omenon, and yet, you must be, otherwise you would not be here."

Isabelle, not as cautious as she should have been, felt no compulsion to kzep quiet. In fact, she was relieved to talk to someone. So, the words tumbled out.

"My name is Isabelle. My father is Dr. Roswell Dvorak. I guess you knew him as Lester Brannon? He used to work here. Apparently, he's the threat. Since he's out of Omenon's reach, I'm the bait to bring him back to Vedanta."

"Ah, Brannon! Yes, a good man. I knew him from his work in the archive during the short time he was here. I could tell he was not cut out for a group like Omenon. I was not surprised when he left the church."

"If you've been working on Project Mind Fuhrer, you must know what's going on around here," Isabelle said.

"I will tell you, since I can't get into more trouble than I'm already in. I am a German scientist. I worked for Herr Hitler on the original Project Mind Fuhrer during the war. We failed to perfect the project

before the Allies, shall we say, 'requisitioned' most of our scientists. The Soviets took a number of us as well.

"I went into hiding when the Reich fell, fearful of what the Soviets might do to me. Franticek Drtikol managed to bring me here. Before I knew it, I was working on Project Mind Fuhrer again, this time in California! But the project had a new mission, and Drtikol had a new name.

"Before he became Ananda Vedanta, he'd published a series of stories which he claimed to be true. The stories said that in 1945, we detonated the first Sun Bomb. Worse than that, it blew up the entire planet. I have no memory of that happening, even though I am one of the original project members. But, of course, Vedanta explained all that. It is due to a case of collective amnesia, he said."

Isabelle Dvorak interrupted Blaupunkt's story.

"If what Vedanta says is true, how are we still here? Obviously, nothing's changed. The Axis lost the war. I can still remember my childhood before Pearl Harbor."

Ruefully, Blaupunkt shook his head.

"People who know nothing of Omenon doctrine would agree with you," Blaupunkt explained. "A person's memories make up the world as they know it. Simply by looking around, one can see that the Earth is still turning. We can read newspaper accounts of the German surrender in May of 1945.

"This is where Omenon demands a leap of faith. It teaches that a replacement Earth from a parallel dimension filled the void that was left by our destroyed planet. The trauma of that experience, Vedanta explained, triggered our collective amnesia. His science fiction story, 'I Remember Earth!' explains this part of the Omenon cosmology.

"And yet," Blaupunkt continued, "It seems suspicious that only Vedanta remembers the catastrophic event. I don't fully understand that. He also wrote about it in another science fiction story in which his protagonist raises the lost continent of Lemuria using Project Mind Fuhrer. That is what Vedanta intends to do; use the Sun Bomb to raise Lemuria, then crown himself emperor of the world."

"He's insane!" Isabelle yelped.

Blaupunkt nodded slowly. "Ananda Vedanta is a dangerous man, and becoming more dangerous each day. We are still not sure of the Sun Bomb's destructive power. The true test will come this week. If today is Christmas, that means the Sun Bombs will go off within 48 hours. Those were my orders before he locked me up."

38
Comeback Conundrum

Ananda Vedanta sat cross-legged on an Oriental rug with his eyes closed. A dense cloud of imported incense filled the sparse room. This was Level 1, the most secure area of the Omenon bunker. His bony fingers rested on the planchette of his personal Ouija board. The centerpiece was a hand-painted image of a swami fakir that had an uncanny resemblance to Vedanta. Using this board he told Deadbeats how to reclaim their bodies. In return they agreed to do his bidding. He had found many bodies to turn over to them. He called them Freeps.

By Vedanta's order, neophytes slept with their talking boards under their pillows. When they became full-fledged Freeps, their boards were tattooed on their backs.

Outwardly, Vedanta preached freedom from the flesh-craving Deadbeats. In reality, he turned his followers into Comebacks.

Transformations begin with The Purge, where neophytes became fertile ground for a Deadbeat takeover. While the neophyte was "riding the board," a term coined by Vedanta to describe an Ouija board session, the Deadbeat slipped in.

Today the Deadbeat inside Vedanta's board was Adolf Hitler. Hitler discovered Vedanta's portal and demanded entry. He had plans for a Fourth Reich.

"What is the problem?" the former Fuhrer sputtered. "Where is my suitable body? You have brought back my best scientists and yet you waste them on frivolous projects that will never succeed. Wake up and smell the bratwurst, Drtikol! Only I can win. I am the genius who will succeed in all things."

"That's your opinion," Vedanta said, projecting his thoughts to the interspatial plane where Hitler's Deadbeat wandered aimlessly. "The way I see it, Divine guidance and my infallible methods will make my plan succeed where yours has failed."

"Listen, *dummkopf*," Hitler screeched, "there can be only one Fuhrer and that's me! This Mind Fuhrer baloney is nothing more than Allied hogwash. I want my Comeback! Now!"

"I think we're finished here," Vedanta announced, lifting the planchette from the board. "I have an appointment for an ear hair trim."

Inside Omenon's underground laboratory, Regis Toomey finished assembling the eighth, and final, Sun Bomb. Each unit would be turned over to Vedanta's Galactic Sea Rangers for installation. The Sea Rangers would then divide themselves into groups and place the units in pre-determined locations.

A Sea Ranger in a deep-sea diver's suit would activate the timer on each unit. The southernmost site was off the Monterey coast. Other bombs lined up along Vedanta's theoretical map of Lemuria.

"I'm worried, Herr Toomey," Heermark Graf, said. "What if we..." Toomey held up his hand to silence him.

"No more defeatist talk, Heermark!" Toomey shuddered. "Lemuria will rise again, and so shall we. This time we must believe unfailingly in Mind Fuhrer's divine wisdom. *Yah?*"

39
The Bunker

I stashed the spider inside the Professor's tin of Half and Half pipe tobacco and slipped it into his shirt pocket. Once inside the bunker the spider would go to work. It was a thin plot, but Vedanta's bunch of mindless minions had us outgunned. It was the only plan we had. Without the spider, we'd be as dead as silent pictures.

Paloma and the Chief would remain at the office as backup. Stan Raycraft returned to his mulled wine beat at the *Call-Bulletin*.

I was so familiar with the road to Pt. Reyes I could have done it with my eyes closed. I turned left at the sign pointing to Inverness, where a dark blue Chrysler got on our tail. This time, they wouldn't let me out of their sight. Leaving the hamlet of Inverness, we turned up Mt. Vision Road.

I counted two Chryslers and a Dodge on our tail now, all dark blue and full of glassy-eyed Freeps. As coastal oaks thickened overhead, our daylight began to fade.

"We're getting close to the bunker now," the Professor said. "You can't miss it."

He was right. The place was crawling with Galactic Rangers, All Knowing Ones, and Freeps ready to welcome Dvorak back into the fold. They did not look friendly. I pulled the Hudson into a turnout off the road, where a group of Rangers surrounded us.

"*Oust!*" one of them barked in Kraut.

I opened the car door. A burly Ratzi yanked me out, spun me around, and frisked me. I'd anticipated this and purposely left Old Betsy at the office. No way would I let the Axis soil my trusty Police Special. Another of the guru's gunsels frisked the Professor. He found the tobacco tin, took it out of his coat pocket and sniffed it.

"You won't be needing this," the Ranger snarled, and tossed the tin on the ground. The lid popped open and shreds of tobacco littered the ground. Our goose was cooked, but good.

They marched us into the woods to an imposing structure straight out of the Mayan jungles. It made the fortress of Ming the Merciless look like an outhouse. It had concrete walls five feet thick behind granite stone blocks. Above it hovered Omenon's iconic symbol: a swastika masquerading as a spinning atom. It floated, suspended by who-knows-what, in mid-air.

Standing where a drawbridge should have been, stood all seven feet of Ananda Vedanta—the Deplorable One himself.

"Mr. Brannon! Or should I say, Professor Dvorak! Welcome home. We've missed you," Vedanta greeted, almost as if he meant it.

"Where's my daughter?" demanded Dvorak.

"All in good time, Professor, all in good time. First, let's have some tea and a chat. I have a handcrafted Mendocino blend that arrived this morning by carrier pigeon."

The guru turned his putrid puss in my direction.

"And this must be the famous, or should I say infamous, Alexander Blade," he sneered like sour milk. I got the feeling I wasn't invited to his tea party. "You have become quite a nuisance, Mr. Blade. Here at Omenon, we have guaranteed methods for overcoming life's challenges. Big and small, the hurdles that life throws across your path are easily overcome through our scientifically-proven methods."

"Great," I replied. "You're my biggest problem; how do I overcome you?"

"There are Norms, like yourself, who don't realize they have a problem until they are forced to confront it," Vedanta blathered. "Seeing as how you're a hostile candidate, you'll find the accommodations on Level 3 better suited for your current state of awareness."

That's when the Prof and I were separated. A pair of Galactic Rangers took me in one direction, and Vedanta took the Prof by the arm and disappeared in another. Did I mention that our goose was cooked?

40
A Welcome Stowaway

Stan Raycraft fiddled with the lock inside the Hudson's trunk. Instead of returning to the *Call-Bulletin* as he said he would, he'd climbed into the trunk of my car. The Galactic Rangers were so busy with myself and the Professor, they didn't bother to check the trunk.

Opening an automobile's trunk from the inside was a useful skill. Stan got some of his best stories by hitching rides in the trunks of cars, and he was determined to get the scoop on Omenon. He opened the lid an inch at a time until he had a clear view of his surroundings. He saw no one. Stealthily, he slipped out, his back to the car, alert for any sign of movement.

Edging his way toward the passenger door, Stan noticed a can of Half and Half pipe tobacco that littered the ground.

"Pssst, hey, Inebriated One, I'm down here," a squeaky voice inside Stan's head beckoned. "Watch where you step. It's me, Sus sistinnako, Thought Spider to you. Pick up the shredded leaf container. I'm inside."

It was a strangely familiar voice, and comforting to Raycraft, who was beginning to reconsider the prudence of his hasty plan.

"Hey, crazy spider cat, is that you?"

"Didn't I just say it was me? C'mon, pick up the can, and put it in your pocket. Be careful!"

Stan looked around. The coast was still clear. It was safe enough to peek inside the Half and Half tin.

"Hey, spidery one, how's it going in there?' Stan asked.

"Silence!" the spider said. "Two hostiles coming this way! Quick, put me in your pocket, and act confused. That shouldn't be difficult. I'll do the talking."

"Whatever you say," Stan replied. "You're the all-knowing one."

The hostiles, two of Vedanta's Galactic Rangers, were returning to their post on Mt. Vision Road when their Aryan peepers landed on the distraught reporter.

"You! Halt!" One of them ordered with Nazi panache. Stan froze. The gunsels approached with Lugers drawn, aimed at his midsection.

"You are trespassing," the ranking gunsel said. "State your purpose here."

A sudden, glazed look in the Rangers' ice blue optics told Stan the spider was already at work. Instead of Stan Raycraft, ace reporter, the gunsels thought they were standing in front of their glorious Mind Fuhrer.

"Thank you for being so cautious, Rangers, but your weapons will not be necessary," the spider projected. "Take me to the Lemurian Reconstruction Room. I do not wish to be seen by anyone. Do you understand?"

"Yawohl, Mind Fuhrer," the taller gunsel yapped. "We will do as you say."

"Good man," the spider purred smugly.

The Rangers shouldered their weapons, glanced at their surroundings, and made for the Lemurian Reconstruction Room.

"Follow us, Mind Fuhrer," the ranger said. "We will get you inside undetected."

Stan Raycraft could not believe his eyes. That he should be mistaken for Ananda Vedanta was nothing less than witchcraft of the highest order.

To the spider, Stan whispered: "Tell me, spidery one. What happens next?"

"Just follow my lead," the spider squeaked. "I know this place inside and out. I drew up the blueprints."

The Lemurian Reconstruction Room was down a long corridor on Level 2. The corridor walls leaned in toward the ceiling, giving it the look of a concrete mineshaft.

The mind-controlled Rangers whisked Stan unseen through various checkpoints. One ranger would distract the guard while the other Ranger guided Stan behind and through the checkpoint. The Lemurian Room was unlocked. Except for Vedanta's private office, all doors in the bunker complex were unlocked. With so many rangers on guard, there was no need to lock them.

"Thank you, that will be all," the spider said to the smartly dressed rangers. "Return to your post and remember nothing of this incident. Understand?"

"*Yahwohl*, Mind Fuhrer!" They clicked their heels together and were gone.

The main feature of the Lemurian Reconstruction Room was a mahogany conference table that was longer than a preacher's sermon. A large map of the mythical Lemuria covered one wall. The spider was obviously proud of the room's design.

"What do you think of the digs?" it asked Stan.

"This is some crazy crib, man! But what's with the Lemuria thing? Don't they know it's a figment of a certain science fiction writer's imagination?"

"Well, you know that, and I know that, but Freeps can't get enough of it," the spider sniffed. "Lemuria is a state of mind, so raising it, and returning to the good old days, if there were any, is what it's all about. The point is, anything is possible, so, why not Lemuria? It has nothing to do with your so-called reality. Earth creatures can't even agree on what that is!"

"I guess not," Stan acquiesced, though still not convinced.

"Once I get Vedanta under my control," the spider said, "I'll halt Project Mind Fuhrer before it detonates my fuel supply."

The spider began spinning a telaug to locate Vedanta. Using its remote viewing feature, the spider found Vedanta and two Rangers inside the dungeon on Level 3.

41
The Spider in Charge

The jailer's key ring jangled in the lock as he opened the cellblock door. Isabelle Dvorak heard the turnkey and leapt from her mattress to the bars of her cell. Having watched her share of prison movies, she pulled out the mirror from her compact and stuck it through the bars to see who was coming.

"Alex!" she yelled, "I'm down here!"

I pushed aside the guard but was shoved back.

"Don't be so impatient, Mr. Blade," the sanctimonious sultan snarled. "Your beautiful client isn't going anywhere. You'll be a happily reunited as soon as your cell is ready. Ah, I'm told it is. Follow me, please?"

The ranger led me to an opened cell next to Grundig Blaupunkt and shoved me inside.

"Please accept our humble lodgings, Mr. Blade," Vedanta said. "I'm sure you've seen worse. Now, if you'll excuse me, I must get back to the good doctor. Oh, and Happy New Year. Hahahaha!"

For a has-been pulp writer, he sure was full of himself. The steel door clanged shut and the guard and Vedanta exited the cell block. All was silent, and that gave us time to compare notes.

"So much for my swell plan, Isabelle," I said. "My ace in the hole is probably a grease spot on the sole of a Nazi's loafers by now."

Despite my troubling assessment, Isabelle's mind was somewhere else. She rattled off a list of grievances, from the lousy prison food to a lack of toiletries and cocktails. When she'd finished ranting she slumped onto her mattress in a depressed funk.

"If you don't mind my saying so," a German accent broke in, "none of this will concern us much longer. Project Mind Fuhrer is about to complete its mission."

Grundig Blaupunkt, rogue Nazi scientist, crushed the last of his Camel under the toe of his shoe.

"If the project is a success," Blaupunkt said placidly, "Vedanta will rule the world. If the project is a failure, as it was in 1945, the world will cease to exist. Simple, *yah?*"

• • •

Stan Raycraft studied the detailed map that hung on the bunker wall. He was as close to sober as he had been last Easter.

"I can't help it, Thought Spider," Raycraft mused, referring to Vedanta's plan for Lemuria. "How does he know Lemuria's even down there?"

"Because I told him it was," the spider said.

"You told him? And you know it's there because…?"

The spider was beginning to prefer Raycraft's drunken self to the sober one.

"Here's the thing," the spider replied impatiently. "You keep forgetting that I wrote 'Quo Valis.' A mythical lost island has gobs of potential for action, political upheaval, explosions, and plenty of them. It makes great pulp fiction, get it? It's better than so-called real life on this sorry planet. Now, do me a favor. Go to that bookshelf next to the portrait of the goofy guru."

The painting Spider was referring to was of Ananda Vedanta clutching a bundle of wheat sheaves in the middle of a vast wheat field at sunrise. The artist painted a benevolent grin on his mug, unlike real life.

"You see that little statue on the third shelf, next to the painting?" the spider said. "Wrap your paws around that statue and pull."

Raycraft reached up and pulled. The statue easily moved forward on a hinge. At that, a hidden door slid upward, taking the portrait with it.

Apparently, the spider had designed a maze of hidden passageways throughout the bunker, an idea it got from reading *Dungeons of the Doomed and Other Tales* magazine. The passages connected all rooms, including Vedanta's fortified office.

Raycraft was overjoyed. "This is wild, daddy-o! A secret passage, just like 'Torchy Blane in Chinatown'!"

"Here's the plan," the spider said. "We'll corner Vedanta in his den and have him recall those bombs before he detonates them. Now, bring that shredded leaf container over here. I'm climbing back in."

Ever so carefully Raycraft placed the tobacco tin, lid open, on the conference table. The spider crawled inside. The reporter picked up the tin, slipped it into a pocket of his Eisenhower jacket, and said:

"Lead the way, space spider."

The journey was circuitous and dark, though every twenty feet or so, a bare electric bulb glowed dimly from the ceiling. On the way, they passed a sliding door connecting to another room. Stan heard voices. It made him nervous, until the spider mentally responded to his concern.

"They don't know we're in here. Besides, I'm using my cloaking ray. We're almost

"I'm a peace-loving cat. No need for the heavy artillery!"

to Vedanta's office now. The Professor's with him."

Seated at his desk, Ananda Vedanta was making notations on the printout from a lie detector machine hooked up to Dvorak, who had been strapped to a chair. The sound of a wall panel swishing open caught Vedanta's attention. A portrait of him sitting on a giant lotus flower rose up into the wall.

Stan Raycraft stood frozen in semi darkness, gaping at the infamous seven-foot guru. Vedanta focused on Raycraft and roared:

"Infidel! You have entered my holiest of holies! This is blasphemy!"

He reached for the intercom on his desk to alert the guards outside his door. But before his finger touched the button, Vedanta heard a familiar squeak inside his scruffy cranium. His hand froze in mid air above the intercom.

"Remember me, Drtikol? I've come back from the grave to see you."

Blood drained from Vedanta's puss. His chin whiskers froze and his eyes glazed over. He couldn't understand how this familiar voice was coming from the stranger inside the secret panel. The voice continued to taunt him.

"It's me, your secret muse, Drtikol. Why did you do it? Why did you bury me in that cemetery? I didn't even rate a funeral after all I've done for you."

Vedanta's voice finally found its way out of his throat.

"Sus sistinnako! I, uh, n-no one knew what happened to you. We thought you'd gone back to your home planet."

"Oh, please," the spider scoffed. "You can do better than that! Have you forgotten I can read your mind? You're trying to hide your thoughts from me, but you're not doing a very good job."

"It doesn't matter," Vedanta said, regaining his composure. "Project Mind Fuhrer has already begun. Soon Lemuria and its ancient technology will be mine. Once I've been crowned Emperor of the World, I'll be more than happy to send you on your way to wherever you wish to go."

"You're padding your part, Drtikol," the spider admonished. "It's too late for that. I want that plutonium and I want it now!"

In a last ditch try to save himself, Vedanta touched a button under his desk with his toe and yelped: "Cross the Rubicon!" Which was Omenon code for "All hands on deck!" A gaggle of Galactic Rangers burst into the room, weapons drawn, aimed directly at Stan Raycraft.

"Hey, hold on fellas," Raycraft sputtered. "I'm a peace-loving cat. No need for that heavy artillery!"

"Drop your weapons!" the spider commanded, using its Unktomian thought ray. "They are red hot coals, burning your fingers!"

In an instant, the rangers dropped their Lugers and began waving their hands in the air like a bunch of holy rollers.

"Before you leave us," the spider said, "untie the Professor, and don't forget to close the door behind you. Now, where was I? Oh, right. I want that plutonium, Drtikol!"

Vedanta sat calmly in his swivel chair behind his whalebone desk, clasping his hands on the desk blotter.

"Let's make a deal," he said to the spider as sweat beaded on his pale forehead.

"Okay, let's," the spider said. "Here's the deal. You call your Sea Rangers and tell them to sail back out and haul up those Sun Bombs. You need to defuse them."

"I can't do that," Vedanta protested. "They've already been set to go off at midnight, that's barely twelve hours from now. There are eight of them, and one's as far south as Monterey."

"Then you don't have much time. Let me give you a little encouragement."

"No, NO, not THAT," Vedanta screeched.

The guru was an automaton staring vacantly

Thought Spider focused its mind ray on Vedanta's nerve centers, taking complete control of his being. The guru was now an automaton staring vacantly at Stan Raycraft.

"Let's get moving," the spider barked at Vedanta's soulless form. "Get on your blow horn and tell your minions to get out there and retrieve those Sun Bombs!"

Vedanta's hand jerked above the intercom, as if an invisible string yanked it into the air. His hand lowered gently, then flicked a switch.

"Barsoom, get in here," Vedanta droned mechanically.

Barsoom Putfarken, captain of the Galactic Rangers, marched into the room, clicked his heels, and waited for the vapid guru's command. Putfarken wore the colorful red and black uniform of the Galactic Guard. He stood six foot five, but that included the heels on his jackboots. Putfarken looked every inch the SS officer he had been during the Third Reich. Glancing suspiciously at Stan Raycraft, a frown clouded his Aryan mug.

"Never mind him, Putfarken," the spider said with Vedanta's vocal cords. "I want all eight Sun Bombs deactivated and returned to me before the clock strikes midnight. Got that?"

"But, Mind Fuhrer, we were about to raise Lemuria with those bombs."

"Silence! I want them returned to me, understand? Take as many men as you need and launch the fleet. There's no time to lose. Get going!"

"Yawohl, Mind Fuhrer!" Putfarken again clicked his heels, spun around and marched out the door.

Stan Raycraft exhaled after Putfarken's departure.

"That cat is a real dead pigeon," Stan said as he watched him leave. "Listen, crazy spider, what happened to my pal Buster Blade, and the Professor's daughter?"

"Not to worry," the spider replied calmly. "They've been detained in the Level 3 dungeon, along with Grundig Blaupunkt, a former Nazi scientist. See that sign above your head?"

Stan craned his neck, gawking at the concrete wall behind him. A large yellow arrow with stenciled white letters read: DUNGEON. The arrow pointed down.

"Can you beat that," Raycraft smiled. "You thought of everything."

"I'm willing to bet Ananda Vedanta will grant a full pardon to your friends," the spider said jovially. "Let's go find out."

The guru was as sullen as he was ashen gray. Subdued by the spider's mind ray, he was under the arachnid's spell but could do nothing about it.

"Let's go, Drtikol," Thought Spider ordered. "You lead the way." The Professor and the addled reporter will follow."

The lanky cult leader lowered his head to avoid hitting it on the ceiling. Raycraft grabbed an emergency flashlight from a niche on the wall, snapped it on, and the three began their descent. Two levels later, the trio came to the dungeon's secret panel. Raycraft pulled a lever that opened a sliding door.

"Hey, Big Daddy, guess who?" Raycraft yelped in my direction.

"How in H did you get here?" I said.

"I hitched a ride in the trunk of your jalopy. Then I found the crazy spider cat laid out on the ground next to your car. We kinda teamed up. The spider does the mental stuff and I do the heavy lifting."

"What I meant was, how'd you get into this cellblock?"

"Oh, yeah," Raycraft replied. "Through a secret passage."

Then I spied Vedanta, standing directly behind Stan.

"What's he doing here? He just locked me up!"

"My friend here," the spider said, referring to Vedanta, "is returning my plutonium. It's a nice gesture, considering the trouble he's put me through. He wants to send me on my way after he releases you and the Professor's daughter. And Blaupunkt. Why not him too?"

Speaking for Vedanta, the spider yelped: "Call the guard!"

Vedanta shuffled to the door to speak with the guard through the small, barred window. The guard, surprised to see his leader on the other side of the cellblock door, opened it in haste. The spider took over from there.

"Unlock the cells," the spider ordered, using Vedanta's voice. "All of them!" The guard obeyed.

42
Ticking Time Bomb

Galactic Seaman Borfred Schwarzman hauled the Sun Bomb to the surface of Tomales Bay. The bomb was small, and resembled a bloated anchor. It weighed only 20 pounds, nothing like the Fat Man and Big Boy atom A-bombs dropped in 1945.

Horst Decker accompanied Schwarzman. The two Omenon sailors had taken the fishing boat *Pt. Reyes* to retrieve the bomb, and now that it was safely aboard, Schwarzman was hungry.

He turned to Decker. "What do you say we head to Bodega Bay for a lunch at Spud Point Fish and Chips?"

Horst Decker was hungry, too, but not hungry enough to disobey the Mind Fuhrer.

"I don't know, Borfred, the Mind Fuhrer wants these bombs returned to the bunker before midnight. He was very clear about that."

"For Pete's sake, it's only two o'clock, Horst," Schwarzman replied. "We have a full tank of fuel, and a good tail wind. We'll be back in plenty of time."

"A crab sandwich does sound good," Decker mumbled.

"It's settled then. Set course for Spud Point."

The Pt. Reyes sliced through the calm waters of Tomales Bay, and within 15 minutes had reached open water. They followed the coastline to Bodega Bay and were tying up at the Spud Point pier within an hour. Shutting down the boat's diesel engine, they climbed up on the pier and headed to the Spud Point Fish and Chips.

Two crab sandwiches, a shrimp cocktail, three beers, and a game of dominoes later, Horst Decker glanced at the ship's clock on the wall. It was already five o'clock.

"Borfred!" Decker yelped. "Look at the time! Let's get going or we'll end up on the receiving end of an Ex-Lax Energizer."

The seamen laid their money on the table, slid back their chairs, and after a brisk walk to the pier, were aboard the *Pt. Reyes*.

All was as they had left it, except for one thing. No Sun Bomb. Someone had taken it. The two seamen pondered their sorry lot in life.

"Horst, this is terrible. This is awful! We have to find that bomb! It does resemble an anchor, and it is crab season. Maybe a someone took it to use as a weight for his crab pots."

"But where do we begin to look, Borfred?"

"Good question," Borfred replied. "Maybe we should call headquarters for further instructions."

"DON'T DO THAT," Horst cringed. "Let's look around the marina first."

"Yes, but if a fisherman took it, it is likely at sea by now. Let's go to the harbormaster's office to find out which boats have set out within the last two hours."

"Good thinking, Borfred."

43
Half Past Satan

Our party had grown to include the Professor, Isabelle, Stan, Ananda Vedanta, Grundig Blaupunkt, myself, and the spider. We decided it would be safer in Vedanta's office. From there, we could monitor the return of the eight sun bombs as they came in.

Vedanta kept a stash of Havana cigars, Vat 69, and clove cigarettes in his office, though I've never been a fan of clove.

The spider stationed Stan next to the blackboard on the office wall. As each bomb came in, Stan made a check on the blackboard, noting its former location and the time of return. At half past ten that night, Stan checked the Santa Cruz and Monterey Sun Bombs from the list. That upped the total to seven, and the spider was not pleased.

"Where's Tomales Bay?" the spider squeaked to no one in particular. "Tomales Bay should have been the first bomb to be returned, not the last!"

A message crackled over the marine band of Vedanta's shortwave radio. The call came from Seaman Decker.

"Pt. Reyes calling the bunker, come in bunker. Over."

The Professor picked up the microphone and flicked a switch.

"Bunker to *Pt. Reyes*, where is your cargo? Over."

"There's been a problem, bunker. We are in pursuit of a fishing boat that stole our cargo, and may have used it to anchor its crab pots. Over."

The spider ordered Vedanta to walk to the microphone. With puppet-like motions he bent down to the microphone. Using Vedanta's vocal cords, the spider barked: "I don't know how you managed to lose that bomb, Decker, but you have less than ninety minutes to deactivate it. Where's that fishing boat? Over."

"I can see it through my binoculars. It's anchored off Pt. Tomales, and it's pulling up its crab pots. We're closing in. Over."

"Get that bomb, you numbskull! And contact me as soon as you have it safely on board. Over."

"Yes, Mind Fuhrer. Over."

No one had seen the spider this agitated, alternating color between violet and purple. It needed a fly to calm itself. The bunker was conspicuously flyless. The vacant vessel that once was Frantichek Drtikol drooled from the corners of his kisser.

It was time to give the home office a call, where I assumed Paloma and the Chief were holding a vigil for our return. I used Vedanta's personal line.

"Moon Cakes, is that you?"

"It's about time you called, Alex. It's nearly midnight. I was about to call St. James to tell him you were in trouble."

"Angel, we've got a situation here with a missing atom bomb, but, fingers crossed, it'll turn up any minute and everything will be jake."

"That doesn't sound like a sure thing, Alex. Hang on, the Chief wants to speak with you."

"Put him on," I said.

"That you, white eyes? Chief got nasty hunch, hot off press. Hunch say get out of there pronto, and don't forget Thought Spider. Chief say big trouble brewing in Pt. Reyes."

"Okay, I'll let the spider know. Thanks, Chief."

Paloma got back on the wire.

"Alex, what the Chief says and get a move on."

"Don't fret, Kitten, see you soon. I think." I hung up the phone and turned to the group.

"We have an urgent message from the Chief," I announced. "We are in a boatload of cow dung and we need to leave. That's all he had to say."

The spider chimed: "In that case, we'd better take the bombs we already have to my ship. It's waiting behind the bunker in a small cave. Seven should give me enough juice to reach a filling station on the way to ERB-46. I'll have some Freeps transport the bombs. It won't take long to convert them to an acceptable fuel for an Unktomian starship. Mine takes ethyl, but regular will do in a pinch."

Vedanta's command went out through a loud speaker in the Freep barracks. Within minutes a gaggle of frantic Freeps was loading bombs into wheelbarrows. Vedanta stood there like a tree stump watching. Stan, the Prof, Isabelle, and I were heading to the Hudson to drive back to Frisco, when a dark blue Chrysler pulled up with Galactic Seamen Horst Decker and Borfred Schwarzman inside. Decker sprinted to the bunker with the final Sun Bomb.

Out of breath, he panted: "Mind Fuhrer, we have the bomb!"

"Good work!" the spider said through Vedanta. "Give it to me."

Horst handed the bomb to Vedanta, who examined it closely. A strange look crossed his pallid pan.

"This bomb hasn't been deactivated!" Vedanta screeched. "Why hasn't it been deactivated?"

"Mind Fuhrer, we are sorry," Schwarzman whined, "It was damaged when the fisherman dropped it overboard. It must have hit a rock."

If the spider had a face, it would have looked horrified. Vedanta turned to Grundig Blaupunkt who stood nearby.

"Blaupunkt," the spider yelped through Vedanta's voice box, "get over here and shut this thing off, or we'll all be incinerated!"

Grundig snatched the bomb from the frantic guru to assess the damage. I glanced at my strap watch.

"We're running out of time. By my watch we're half past Satan," I said. "That's who's in our future if Dr. Blaupunkt can't stop this thing. No pressure, doc, just saying."

The trunk was empty

Glancing at the frantic crowd surrounding him, Blaupunkt pleaded: "Does anyone have a Phillips screwdriver?"

I dashed to the Hudson where I kept an emergency toolbox in the trunk. I flung open the lid. The trunk was empty! Then I remembered. The Chief borrowed my tool kit to take apart the office TV. It's back at the office.

I have a new motto: Never loan your tools.

"Oh, brother." I almost said.

44
Déjà vu?

Santa and his eight tiny reindeer were circling San Francisco like hookers at a Shriners' convention. And, like every Christmas, private snoops were about as popular as a last minute stocking stuffer. Instead of soaking up holiday cheer like everyone else, I was on a skip trace job in the Tenderloin, scraping up this month's payment for our new office television.

Me? I hate TV, but my partner, Paloma Liu Tsong can't get enough of it. You'd think a Hastings Law School grad like Paloma would dig high culture. You know, like the art collection at the DeYoung Museum, or opera at Davies Symphony Hall, stuff like that.

I know what you're thinking. What's a brainy bundle of curves with a rack like hers doing with an outfit like Confidential Investigations? Simple. She got bored with the District Attorney's office. Too stifling, she said. She craved adventure, the street, life, death, and everything in between.

She also likes to think she's the brains of this outfit. But guess what? The door's still got my name on it: Alexander Blade, Private Investigator. I let her think she's the big draw, which I admit, she is with the male clients. They go gaga for her.

Anyway, after dodging frantic Christmas shoppers all day, I was ankling down Turk Street when I passed the Salvation Army's Tenderloin station. Their Army brass band was belting out Christmas favorites to the frantic shoppers.

"Hey, Buster!" a familiar voice shouted over the din. Stan Raycraft, the band's tambourine man, waved me over. He'd checked himself into the Army nine months ago to dry out. He said the stress of newspaper work had him writing stories from the bottom of a bottle. One day he decided to give up the booze.

"Hey, Stan. Merry Christmas." I shouted over the music. "Long time no see, buddy. How've you been?"

"Nine months and still sober, man," Stan said. "It's a whole new world."

"Well, keep it up, and drop by the office sometime. Paloma would love to see you before the New Year."

"Will do, Big Daddy!"

As I waited for the stoplight to change, I noticed I was only a block from police headquarters, where Lieutenant Leroy St. James heads up the homicide squad. He didn't get a copy of our agency Christmas newsletter this year, due to our broken mimeograph machine. I thought I'd make up for the mishap and drop by to spread a little cheer.

As I approached St. James' office, the notes of an Italian opera tickled my ears, Rossini's "Barber of Seville," if I wasn't mistaken. It came from St. James's portable phonograph. I opened the door and strolled in.

"Blade! You've been as scarce as a hen's tooth," the jolly homicide honcho crowed. "I'm sure glad you dropped in. I need your advice on the Blanche Meriwether case. It's been a tough one. There are way too many suspects, and every one of them had a motive for murder. I suppose you've read about it in the papers?"

"Indeed I have, Lieutenant," I said. "Blanche's Reiki therapist did it, and he's purchased a ticket on the steamer Capistrano, bound for Argentina tonight. Better hurry."

"Good gawd almighty!" St. James gasped. "Why's it always the one you least suspect? I should know that by now! I owe you one, Buster. I'll put out an APB on the Reiki perp right now."

"Oh," I prattled, "by the way. I haven't seen you since you got hitched to your Hollywood heartthrob. Congratulations. I guess the little woman will be burning up the 101 between here and Hollywood to keep up her hectic shooting schedule."

"Aw, well, you know Gene Tierney, I mean, Gene St. James," the lieutenant corrected apologetically. "She's a driven woman, and as long as they keep offering her good roles, she won't unpack the suitcase."

• • •

Next day at the office...

We were desperate. While conjuring an Ouija board on a new case, we accidentally awakened the spirit of Little Pete, the treacherous, lecherous, Chinese gangster from Chinatown's Victorian era.

We were on our way to meet an authentic tribal Chief by the name of Joseph Iron Lung, a Cambridge scholar and the world's authority on Native American mysticism. Scuttlebutt had the Chief staying at the St. Francis Hotel, and our source was correct.

We were about to inform the desk clerk of the purpose of our visit when the desk phone jingled. The clerk listened to the caller at the other end of the wire.

"Yes, they're here," the clerk said, gazing vacantly our way. He hung up the phone and asked: "Are you Alexander Blade?"

"Why yes, how'd you..." Before I could finish, the clerk said, "Chief Iron Lung says he will see you. His room is 502. Elevators are on your left."

I looked at Paloma. "How the heck did he know we were here?" I asked. "He doesn't know us from Adam and Eve."

We took the elevator to the fifth floor, found Room 502 and knocked. The Chief answered the door himself. He cut quite a figure in his double-breasted Brooks Brothers suit. He looked every inch the CEO of an oil company, which, my source confirmed, he was. His tribe was pumping crude near Petrolia, on the Lost Coast. He bowed and offered us a seat. We sat on a plush sofa in his two-room suite and presented our case.

Chief showed interest. "Mr. Blade, Miss Tsong, if you think I can be of help, I will gladly offer my services."

"We'll be happy to pay your regular rates," Paloma offered.

"I wouldn't think of it!" the Chief replied. "These exorcisms help me with my research. I'm working on a book about Native American ritual in Humboldt County. Your uninvited guest will give me the opportunity to use some of the more arcane rituals of my ancestors. I've been wanting to try them out on a challenging case."

With a renewed sense of hope, we bid farewell to the Chief and climbed aboard the cable car heading uphill to Grant Avenue. I didn't mention it to Paloma, but I'd had this weird feeling all day, as if everything we'd been through the last few days had happened before. It all seemed so familiar. But, it must have been my imagination. Everyone knows that Christmas comes but once a year.

THE AUTHOR

Richard Toronto is an American-born writer and science-fiction historian best known for his detailed chronicling of the controversial "Shaver Mystery" and its central figures, Richard S. Shaver and Raymond A. Palmer.

Born in Sonoma, California, Toronto earned a BA in Journalism from CSU Sacramento. He taught film photography to patients at Napa State Hospital for the Criminally Insane. He was a newspaper reporter for a small Bay Area daily, and founded Shavertron—"Your Only Source of Post-Deluge Shaverania"—publishing 29 issues, the longest run of any Shaver Mystery-related fanzine.

Toronto's work is rooted in pulp-era science fiction history and the preservation of esoteric literary subcultures. His narrative blends biography, cultural criticism, and archival research. He began documenting the legacy of fringe sci-fi long before such sub-genres became academically studied.

His detective fiction reflects this pulp era fascination. His debut novel, *Hollywood and Vain*, introduced Alexander "Buster" Blade, a former silent movie child actor turned private detective in postwar San Francisco. The city itself plays a vivid role, blending postwar noir atmosphere tinged with Hollywood McCarthyism.

The series explores post-WWII social dynamics, race, and the emerging detective-fiction tropes in early 20th century California. His bi-racial character, Paloma Liu Tsong, flees small town agricultural life in the Sacramento Delta to become an exotic dancer in the Chinatown club scene. She goes to work for Blade's agency and eventually becomes a private eye in her own novel, *Nudist Camp Confidential.*

Sequels became more genre-bending as the series evolved. *Half Past Satan*, a fast-paced atmospheric novella that takes place in West Marin County, pulls the reader into occult noir and a world where Nazi technology collides with Ouija boards. It merges hard-boiled detective pulp with weird sci-fi/ fantasy, full of 1940s noir slang, tongue-in-cheek humor, and escalating weirdness. The novel is classic mid-century detective fiction with a retro-fantasy twist, exploring philosophical ideas around cults, mysticism, and psychological manipulation. A Goodreads reviewer described *Half Past Satan* as "a sci-fantasy disguised as a detective yarn."

Toronto's books can be found on Amazon.

www.friscodetective.com

www.shavertron.com

httpswww.facebook.com/friscodetective/

https://www.facebook.com/ShavertronPress/

Before You Go:
It is always appreciated when readers leave reviews for our books on Amazon.com. It's the only way a book gets noticed, for ranking on Amazon. Thanks in advance for the review, be it good, bad, or somewhere in the middle.

Marvin D. Fox
Chief, Cook, Bottle Washer,
Atomic Crime Library

www.ingramcontent.com/pod-product-compliance
Lightning Source LLC
Chambersburg PA
CBHW050753250626
47155CB00005B/2038